J. M. (James Matthew) Barrie

The Novels, Tales and Sketches

Sentimental Tommy: Part II

J. M. (James Matthew) Barrie

The Novels, Tales and Sketches
Sentimental Tommy: Part II

ISBN/EAN: 9783337000905

Printed in Europe, USA, Canada, Australia, Japan

Cover: Foto ©Andreas Hilbeck / pixelio.de

More available books at **www.hansebooks.com**

J. M. BARRIE

Vol. VII

SENTIMENTAL TOMMY

THE NOVELS, TALES AND SKETCHES OF J. M. BARRIE 🐦 🐦 🐦

SENTIMENTAL TOMMY

PART II

❦ PUBLISHED IN
NEW YORK BY
CHARLES SCRIBNER'S
SONS ❦ ❦ 1896 ❦

LONDON : HODDER & STOUGHTON

GRIZEL.

Drawn by William Hatherell.

GRIZEL.
Drawn by William Hatherell.

THE NOVELS, TALES AND SKETCHES OF J. M. BARRIE 🐿 🐿 🐿

SENTIMENTAL TOMMY

PART II

🐿 PUBLISHED IN
NEW YORK BY
CHARLES SCRIBNER'S
SONS 🐿 🐿 1896 🐿

LONDON : HODDER & STOUGHTON

AUTHOR'S EDITION

J. M. Barrie

THE DE VINNE PRESS, NEW YORK, U. S. A.

CONTENTS

Part II

v

SENTIMENTAL TOMMY

PART II

CHAPTER XXI

THE LAST JACOBITE RISING

ON the evening of the Queen's birthday, bridies were eaten to her honour in a hundred Thrums homes, and her health was drunk in toddy, Scotch toddy and Highland toddy. Patullo, the writer, gave a men's party, and his sole instructions to his maid were "Keep running back and forrit wi' the hot water." At the bank there was a ladies' party and ginger wine. From Cathro's bedroom-window a flag was displayed with *Vivat Regina* on it, the sentiment composed by Cathro, the words sewn by the girls of his McCulloch class. The eight-o'clock bell rang for an hour, and a loyal crowd had gathered in the square to shout. To a superficial observer, such as the Baron Bailie or Todd, the new policeman, all seemed well and fair.

But a very different scene was being enacted at

261

the same time in the fastnesses of the Den, where three resolute schemers had met by appointment. Their trysting-place was the Cuttle Well, which is most easily reached by the pink path made for that purpose ; but the better to further their dark and sinister design, the plotters arrived by three circuitous routes, one descending the Reekie Broth Pot, a low but dangerous waterfall, the second daring the perils of the crags, and the third walking stealthily up the burn.

" Is that you, Tommy? "

" Whist ! Do you mind the pass-word ? "

" Stroke ! "

" Right. Have you heard Gav Dishart coming ? "

" I hinna. I doubt his father had grippit him as he was slinking out o' the manse."

" I fear it, Corp. I'm thinking his father is in the Woman's pay."

" What woman ? "

" The Woman of Hanover ? "

" That's the queen, is it no ? "

" She'll never get me to call her queen."

" Nor yet me. I think I hear Gav coming."

Gav Dishart was the one who had come by the burn, and his boots were cheeping like a field of mice. He gave the word " Stroke," and the three then looked at each other firmly. The lights of the town were not visible from the Cuttle Well, owing to an arm of cliff that is outstretched between, but the bell could be distinctly heard, and occasionally a shout of revelry.

"They little ken!" said Tommy, darkly.

"They hinna a notion," said Corp, but he was looking somewhat perplexed himself.

"It's near time I was back for family exercise," said Gav, uneasily, "so we had better do it quick, Tommy."

"Did you bring the wineglasses?" Tommy asked him.

"No," Gav said, "the press was lockit, but I've brought egg-cups."

"Stand round then."

The three boys now presented a picturesque appearance, but there was none save the man in the moon to see them. They stood round the Cuttle Well, each holding an egg-cup, and though the daring nature of their undertaking and the romantic surroundings combined to excite them, it was not fear but soaring purpose that paled their faces and caused their hands to tremble, when Tommy said solemnly, "Afore we do what we've come here to do, let's swear."

"Stroke!" he said.

"Stroke!" said Gav.

"Stroke!" said Corp.

They then filled their cups and holding them over the well, so that they clinked, they said:

" To the king ower the water ! "

" To the king ower the water ! "

" To the king ower the water ! "

When they had drunk Tommy broke his cup against a rock, for he was determined that it should never be used to honour a meaner toast, and the others followed his example, Corp briskly, though the act puzzled him, and Gav with a gloomy look because he knew that the cups would be missed to-morrow.

" Is that a' now ? " whispered Corp, wiping his forehead with his sleeve.

" All ! " cried Tommy. " Man, we've just be-good."

As secretly as they had entered it, they left the Den, and anon three figures were standing in a dark trance, cynically watching the revellers in the square.

" If they just kent ! " muttered the smallest, who was wearing his jacket outside in to escape obser-vation.

" But they little ken ! " said Gav Dishart.

" They hinna a notion ! " said Corp, contemp-tuously, but still he was a little puzzled, and pres-ently he asked softly: " Lads, what just is it that they dinna ken ? "

Had Gav been ready with an answer he could not have uttered it, for just then a terrible little man in black, who had been searching for him in likely places, seized him by the cuff of the neck, and, turning his face in an easterly direction, ran him to family worship. But there was still work to do for the other two. Walking home alone that night from Mr. Patullo's party, Mr. Cathro had an uncomfortable feeling that he was being dogged. When he stopped to listen, all was at once still, but the moment he moved onward he again heard stealthy steps behind. He retired to rest as soon as he reached his house, to be wakened presently by a slight noise at the window, whence the flag-post protruded. It had been but a gust of wind, he decided, and turned round to go to sleep again, when crash! the post was plucked from its place and cast to the ground. The dominie sprang out of bed, and while feeling for a light, thought he heard scurrying feet, but when he looked out at the window no one was to be seen; *Vivat Regina* lay ignobly in the gutters. That it could have been the object of an intended theft was not probable, but the open window might have tempted thieves, and there was a possible though risky way up by the spout. The affair was a good deal talked about at the time, but it remained shrouded in a mystery which even we have been unable to penetrate.

On the heels of the Queen's birthday came the Muckley, the one that was to be known to fame, if fame was willing to listen to Corp, as Tommy's

Muckley. Unless he had some grand aim in view never was a boy who yielded to temptations more blithely than Tommy, but when he had such aim never was a boy so firm in withstanding them. At this Muckley he had a mighty reason for not spending money, and with ninepence in his pocket clamouring to be out he spent not one halfpenny. There was something uncanny in the sight of him stalking unscathed between rows of stands and shows, everyone of them aiming at his pockets. Corp and Gav, of course, were in the secret and did their humble best to act in the same unnatural manner, but now and again a show made a successful snap at Gav, and Corp had gloomy fears that he would lose his head in presence of the Teuch and Tasty, from which humiliation indeed he was only saved by the happy idea of requesting Tommy to shout "Deuteronomy!" in a warning voice, every time they drew nigh Californy's seductive stand.

Was there nothing for sale, then, that the three thirsted to buy? There were many things, among them weapons of war, a pack of cards, more properly called Devil's books, blue bonnets suitable for Highland gentlemen, feathers for the bonnets, a tin lantern, yards of tartan cloth, which the deft fingers of Grizel would convert into warriors' sashes. Corp knew that these purchases were in Tommy's far-seeing eye, but he thought the only way to get them was to ask the price and then offer half. Gav, the scholar, who had already reached daylight through the first three books of Euclid, and took a walk every Saturday morning with his father and Herodotus, even Gav, the scholar, was as thick-witted as Corp.

"We'll let other laddies buy them," Tommy explained in his superior way, "and then after the Muckley is past, we'll buy them frae them."

The others understood now. After a Muckley there was always a great dearth of pence, and a moneyed man could become owner of Muckley purchases at a sixth part of the Muckley price.

"You crittur!" exclaimed Corp, in abject admiration.

But Gav saw an objection. "The feck of them," he pointed out, "will waur their siller on shows and things to eat, instead of on what we want them to buy."

"So they will, the nasty sackets!" cried Corp.

"You couldna blame a laddie for buying Teuch and Tasty," continued Gav with triumph, for he was a little jealous of Tommy.

"You couldna," agreed Corp, "no, I'll be dagont, if you could," and his hand pressed his money feverishly.

"Deuteronomy!" roared Tommy, and Corp's hand jumped as if it had been caught in some other person's pocket.

"But how are we to do?" he asked. "If you like, I'll take Birkie and the Haggerty-Taggertys round the Muckley and fight ilka ane that doesna buy —— "

"Corp," said Tommy, calmly, "I wonder at you. Do you no ken yet that the best plan is to leave a' thing to me?"

"Blethering gowks that we are, of course it is!" cried Corp, and he turned almost fiercely upon Gav. "Lippen all to him," he said with grand confidence, "he'll find a wy."

And Tommy found a way. Birkie was the boy who bought the pack of cards. He saw Tommy looking so woe-begone that it was necessary to ask the reason.

"Oh, Birkie, lend me threepence," sobbed Tommy, "and I'll give you sixpence the morn."

"You're daft," said Birkie, "there's no a laddie in Thrums that will have one single lonely bawbee the morn."

"Him that buys the cards," moaned Tommy, "will never be without siller, for you tell auld folks fortunes on them at a penny every throw. Lend me threepence, Birkie. They cost a sic, and I have just —— "

"Na, na," said greedy Birkie, "I'm no to be catched wi' chaff. If it's true, what you say, I'll buy the cards mysel'."

Having thus got hold of him, Tommy led

Birkie to a stand where the King of Egypt was telling fortunes with cards, and doing a roaring trade among the Jocks and Jennys. He also sold packs at sixpence each, and the elated Birkie was an immediate purchaser.

" You're no so clever as you think yoursel'!" he said triumphantly to Tommy, who replied with his inscrutable smile. But to his satellites he said, " Not a soul will buy a fortune frae Birkie. I'll get thae cards for a penny afore next week's out."

Francie Crabb found Tommy sniggering to himself in the back wynd. " What are you goucking at?" asked Francie in surprise, for, as a rule, Tommy only laughed behind his face.

" I winna tell you," chuckled Tommy, " but what a bar, oh, what a divert!"

" Come on, tell me."

" Well, it's at the man as is swallowing swords ahint the menagerie."

" I see nothing to laugh at in that."

" I'm no laughing at that. I'm laughing at him for selling the swords for ninepence the piece. Oh, what ignorant he is, oh, what a bar!"

" Ninepence is a mislaird price for a soord," said Francie. " I never gave ninepence."

Tommy looked at him in the way that always made boys fidget with their fists.

" You're near as big a bar as him," he said

scornfully. "Did you ever see the sword that's hanging on the wall in the backroom at the post-office?"

"No, but my father has telled me about it. It has a grand name."

"It's an Andrea Ferrara, that's what it is."

"Ay, I mind the name now; there has been folk killed wi' that soord."

This was true, for the post-office Andrea Ferrara has a stirring history, but for the present its price was the important thing. "Dr. McQueen offered a pound note for it," said Tommy.

"I ken that, but what has that to do wi' the soord-swallower?"

"Just this; that the swords he is selling for nine-pence are Andrea Ferraras, the same as the post-office one, and he could get a pound a piece for them if he kent their worth. Oh, what a bar, oh, what —— "

Francie's eyes lit up greedily, and he looked at his two silver shillings, and took two steps in the direction of the sword-swallower's, and faltered and could not make up his agitated mind. Tommy set off toward the square at a brisk walk.

"Whaur are you off to?" asked Francie, following him.

"To tell the man what his swords is worth. It would be ill done no to tell him." To clinch the matter, off went Tommy at a run, and off went

Francie after him. As a rule Tommy was the swifter, but on this occasion he lagged of fell purpose, and reached the sword-swallower's tent just in time to see Francie emerge elated therefrom, carrying two Andrea Ferraras. Francie grinned when they met.

"What a bar!" he crowed.

"What a bar!" agreed Tommy, and sufficient has now been told to show that he had found a way. Even Gav acknowledged a master, and, when the accoutrements of war were bought at second hand as cheaply as Tommy had predicted, applauded him with eyes and mouth for a full week, after which he saw things in a new light. Gav of course was to enter the bursary lists anon, and he had supposed that Cathro would have the last year's schooling of him; but no, his father decided to send him for the grand final grind to Mr. Ogilvy of Glen Quharity, a famous dominie between whom and Mr. Dishart existed a friendship that none had ever got at the root of. Mr. Cathro was more annoyed than he cared to show, Gav being of all the boys of that time the one likeliest to do his teacher honour at the university competitions, but Tommy, though the decision cost him an adherent, was not ill-pleased, for he had discovered that Gav was one of those irritating boys who like to be leader. Gav, as has been said, suddenly saw Tommy's victory over Messrs. Birkie,

Francie, etc., in a new light; this was because when he wanted back the shilling which he had contributed to the funds for buying their purchases, Tommy replied firmly:

" I canna give you the shilling, but I'll give you the lantern and the tartan cloth we bought wi' it."

" What use could they be to me at Glenquharity?" Gav protested.

" Oh, if they are no use to you," Tommy said sweetly, "me and Corp is willing to buy them off you for threepence."

Then Gav became a scorner of duplicity, but he had to consent to the bargain, and again Corp said to Tommy, " Oh, you crittur!" But he was sorry to lose a fellow-conspirator. " There's just the twa o' us now," he sighed.

" Just twa!" cried Tommy. " What are you havering about, man? There's as many as I like to whistle for."

" You mean Grizel and Elspeth, I ken, but —— "

" I wasna thinking of the women-folk," Tommy told him, with a contemptuous wave of the hand. He went closer to Corp, and said, in a low voice, " The McKenzies are waiting!"

" Are they, though?" said Corp, perplexed, as he had no notion who the McKenzies might be.

" And Lochiel has twa hunder spearsmen."

" Do you say so?"

" Young Kinnordy's ettling to come out, and I

meet Lord Airlie, when the moon rises, at the Loups o' Kenny, and auld Bradwardine's as spunky as ever, and there's fifty wild Highlandmen lying ready in the muckle cave of Clova."

He spoke so earnestly that Corp could only ejaculate, " Michty me ! "

" But of course they winna rise," continued Tommy, darkly, " till he lands."

" Of course no," said Corp, " but — wha is he ? "

" Himsel'," whispered Tommy, "the Chevalier!"

Corp hesitated. " But, I thought," he said diffidently, " I thought you ——— "

" So I am," said Tommy.

" But you said he hadna landed yet ? "

" Neither he has."

" But you ——— "

" Well ? "

" You're here, are you no ? "

Tommy stamped his foot in irritation. " You're slow in the uptak," he said. " I'm no here. How can I be here when I'm at St. Germains ? "

" Dinna be angry wi' me," Corp begged. " I ken you're ower the water, but when I see you, I kind of forget; and just for the minute I think you're here."

" Well, think afore you speak."

" I'll try, but that's teuch work. When do you come to Scotland ? "

" I'm no sure; but as soon as I'm ripe."

273

At nights Tommy now sometimes lay among the cabbages of the school-house watching the shadow of Black Cathro on his sitting-room blind. Cathro never knew he was there. The reason Tommy lay among the cabbages was that there was a price upon his head.

"But if Black Cathro wanted to get the blood-money," Corp said apologetically, "he could nab you any day. He kens you fine."

Tommy smiled meaningly. "Not him," he answered, "I've cheated him bonny, he hasna a notion wha I am. Corp, would you like a good laugh?"

"That I would."

"Weel, then, I'll tell you wha he thinks I am. Do you ken a little house yont the road a bitty frae Monypenny?"

"I ken no sic house," said Corp, "except Aaron's."

"Aaron's the man as bides in it," Tommy continued hastily, "at least I think that's the name. Well, as you ken the house, you've maybe noticed a laddie that bides there too?"

"There's no laddie," began Corp, "except——"

"Let me see," interrupted Tommy, "what was his name? Was it Peter? No. Was it Willie? Stop, I mind, it was Tommy."

He glared so that Corp dared not utter a word. "Have you notitched him?"

" I've — I've seen him," Corp gasped.

"Well, this is the joke," said Tommy, trying vainly to restrain his mirth, "Cathro thinks I'm that laddie! Ho! ho! ho!"

Corp scratched his head, then he bit his warts, then he spat upon his hands, then he said " Damn."

The crisis came when Cathro, still ignorant that the heather was on fire, dropped some disparaging remarks about the Stuarts to his history class. Tommy said nothing, but — but one of the school-windows was without a snib, and next morning when the dominie reached his desk he was surprised to find on it a little cotton glove. He raised it on high, greatly puzzled, and then, as ever when he suspected knavery, his eyes sought Tommy, who was sitting on a form, his arms proudly folded. That the whelp had put the glove there, Cathro no longer doubted, and he would have liked to know why, but was reluctant to give him the satisfaction of asking. So the gauntlet — for gauntlet it was — was laid aside, the while Tommy, his head bumming like a beeskep, muttered triumphantly through his teeth, " But he lifted it, he lifted it!" and at closing time it was flung in his face with this fair tribute :

" I'm no a rich man, laddie, but I would give a pound note to know what you'll be at ten years from now."

There could be no mistaking the dire meaning

of these words, and Tommy hurried, pale but determined, to the quarry, where Corp, with a barrow in his hands, was learning strange phrases by heart, and finding it a help to call his warts after the new swears.

"Corp," cried Tommy, "I've set sail!"

On the following Saturday evening Charles Edward landed in the Den. In his bonnet was the white cockade, and round his waist a tartan sash; though he had long passed man's allotted span his face was still full of fire, his figure lithe and even boyish. For state reasons he had assumed the name of Captain Stroke. As he leapt ashore from the bark, the Dancing Shovel, he was received right loyally by Corp and other faithful adherents, of whom only two, and these of a sex to which his House was ever partial, were visible, owing to the gathering gloom. Corp of that Ilk sank on his knees at the water's edge, and kissing his royal master's hand said, fervently, " Welcome, my prince, once more to bonny Scotland!" Then he rose and whispered, but with scarcely less emotion, " There's an egg to your tea."

CHAPTER XXII

THE SIEGE OF THRUMS

THE man in the moon is a native of Thrums, who was put up there for hacking sticks on the Sabbath, and as he sails over the Den his interest in the bit placey is still sufficient to make him bend forward and cry "Boo!" at the lovers. When they jump apart you can see the aged reprobate grinning. Once out of sight of the Den, he cares not a boddle how the moon travels, but the masterful crittur enrages him if she is in a hurry here, just as he is cleverly making out whose children's children are courting now. "Slow, there!" he cries to the moon, but she answers placidly that they have the rest of the world to view to-night. "The rest of the world be danged!" roars the man, and he cranes his neck for a last glimpse of the Cuttle Well, until he nearly falls out of the moon.

Never had the man such a trying time as during the year now before him. It was the year when so many scientific magnates sat up half the night in their shirts, spying at him through telescopes. But every effort to discover why he was in such a fidget failed, because the spy-glasses were never levelled at the Thrums Den. Through the whole of the incidents now to tell, you may conceive the man (on whom sympathy would be wasted) dagoning horribly, because he was always carried past the den before he could make head or tail of the change that had come over it.

The spot chosen by the ill-fated Stuart and his gallant remnant for their last desperate enterprise was eminently fitted for their purpose. Being round the corner from Thrums, it was commanded by no fortified place save the farm of Nether Drumgley, and on a recent goustie night nearly all the trees had been blown down, making a hundred hiding-places for bold climbers, and transforming the Den into a scene of wild and mournful grandeur. In no bay more suitable than the flooded field called the Silent Pool could the hunted prince have cast anchor, for the Pool is not only sheltered from observation, but so little troubled by gales that it had only one drawback: at some seasons of the year it was not there. This, however, did not vex Stroke, as it is cannier to call him, for he burned his boats on the night he landed (and a dagont, tedious job it was too), and pointed out to his followers that the drouth which kept him in must also keep the enemy out. Part of the way to the lair they usually traversed in the burn, because water leaves no trace, and though they carried turnip lanterns and were armed to the teeth, this was often a perilous journey owing to the lovers close at hand on the pink path, from which the trees had been cleared, for lads and lasses must walk whate'er betide. Ronny-On's Jean and Peter Scrymgeour, little Lisbeth Doak and long Sam'l from Pyotdykes were pairing that year, and never knew how near they were to being dirked by Corp of Corp, who, lurking in the burn till there were no tibbits in his toes, muttered fiercely, " Cheep one single cheep, and it will be thy hinmost, methinks ! " under the impression that Methinks was a Jacobite oath.

For this voluntary service, Stroke clapped Corp of Corp on the shoulder with a naked sword, and said, " Rise, Sir Joseph ! " which made Corp more confused than ever, for he was already Corp of Corp, Him of Muckle Kenny, Red McNeil, Andrew Ferrara, and the Master of Inverquharity (Stroke's names), as well as Stab-in-the-Dark, Grind-them-to-Mullins, and Warty Joe (his own), and which he was at any particular moment he never knew, till Stroke told him, and even then he forgot and had to be put in irons.

The other frequenters of the lair on Saturday nights (when alone the rebellion was active) were the proud Lady Grizel and Widow Elspeth. It had been thought best to make Elspeth a widow, because she was so religious.

279

The lair was on the right bank of the burn, near the waterfall, and you climbed to it by ropes, unless you preferred an easier way. It is now a dripping hollow, down which water dribbles from beneath a sluice, but at that time it was hidden on all sides by trees and the huge clods of sward they had torn from the earth as they fell. Two of these clods were the only walls of the lair, which had at times a ceiling not unlike Aaron Latta's bed coverlets, and the chief furniture was two barrels, marked " Usquebach " and " Powder." When the darkness of Stroke's fortunes sat like a pall upon his brow, as happened sometimes, he sought to drive it away by playing cards on one of these barrels with Sir Joseph, but the approach of the Widow made him pocket them quickly with a warning sign to his trusty knight, who did not understand, and asked what had become of them, whereupon Elspeth cried, in horror:

"Cards! Oh, Tommy, you promised —— "

But Stroke rode her down with, "Cards! Wha has been playing cards? You, Muckle Kenny, and you, Sir Joseph, after I forbade it! Hie, there, Inverquharity, all of you, seize those men."

Then Corp blinked, came to his senses and marched himself off to the prison on the lonely promontory called the Queen's Bower, saying ferociously, "Jouk, Sir Joseph, and I'll blaw you into posterity."

THE SIEGE OF THRUMS

It is sable night when Stroke and Sir Joseph reach a point in the Den whence the glimmering lights of the town are distinctly visible. Neither speaks. Presently the distant eight-o'clock bell rings, and then Sir Joseph looks anxiously at his warts, for this is the signal to begin, and as usual he has forgotten the words.

"Go on," says someone in a whisper. It cannot be Stroke, for his head is brooding on his breast. This mysterious voice haunted all the doings in the Den, and had better be confined in brackets.

("Go on.")

"Methinks," says Sir Joseph, "methinks the borers —— "

("Burghers.")

"Methinks the burghers now cease from their labours."

"Ay," replied Stroke, "'tis so, would that they ceased from them forever!"

"Methinks the time is at hand."

"Ha!" exclaims Stroke, looking at his lieutenant curiously, "what makest thou say so? For three weeks these fortifications have defied my cannon, there is scarce a breach yet in the walls of yonder town."

"Methinks thou wilt find a way."

"It may be so, my good Sir Joseph, it may be so, and yet, even when I am most hopeful of success, my schemes go a gley."

" Methinks thy dark —— "

(" Dinna say Methinks so often.")

(" Tommy, I maun. If I dinna get that to start me off, I go through other.")

(" Go on.")

" Methinks thy dark spirit lies on thee to-night."

" Ay, 'tis too true. But cans't thou blame me if I grow sad ? The town still in the enemy's hands, and so much brave blood already spilt in vain. Knowest thou that the brave Kinnordy fell last night ? My noble Kinnordy ! "

Here Stroke covers his face with his hands, weeping silently, and — and there is an awkward pause.

(" Go on — ' Still have me.' ")

(" So it is.") " Weep not, my royal scone —— "

(" Scion.")

" Weep not, my royal scion, havest thou not still me ? "

" Well said, Sir Joseph," cries Stroke, dashing the sign of weakness from his face. " I still have many brave fellows, and with their help I shall be master of this proud town."

" And then ghost we to fair Edinburgh ? "

" Ay, 'tis so, but, Sir Joseph, thinkest thou these burghers love the Stuart not ? "

" Nay, methinks they are true to thee, but their starch commander — (give me my time, this is a lang ane,) but their arch commander is thy bitterest foe. Vile spoon that he is! (It's no spoon, it's spawn.)"

" Thou meanest the craven Cathro ? "

" Methinks ay. (I like thae short anes.)"

" 'Tis well !" says Stroke, sternly. " That man hath ever slipped between me and my right. His time will come."

" He floppeth thee — he flouteth thee from the battlements."

" Ha, 'tis well !"

(" You've said that already.")

(" I say it twice.")

(" That's what aye puts me wrang.) Ghost thou to meet the proud Lady Grizel to-night ? "

" Ay."

" Ghost thou alone ? "

" Ay."

(" What easy anes you have !) I fear it is not chancey for thee to go."

" I must dree my dreed."

" These women is kittle cattle."

" The Stuart hath ever a soft side for them. Ah, my trusty foster-brother, knowest thou not what it is to love ? "

" Alas, I too have had my fling. (Does Grizel kiss your hand yet ?) "

" (No, she winna, the limmer.) Sir Joseph, I go to her."

"Methinks she is a haughty onion. I prithee go not to-night."

"I have given my word."

"Thy word is a band."

"Adieu, my friend."

"Methinks thou ghost to thy damn. (Did we no promise Elspeth there should be no swearing?)"

The raft Vick Ian Vohr is dragged to the shore, and Stroke steps on board, a proud solitary figure. "Farewell!" he cries hoarsely, as he seizes the oar.

"Farewell, my leech," answers Corp, and then helps him to disembark. Their hands chance to meet, and Stroke's is so hot that Corp quails.

"Tommy," he says, with a shudder, "do you — you dinna think it's a' true, do you?" But the ill-fated prince only gives him a warning look and plunges into the mazes of the forest. For a long time silence reigns over the Den. Lights glint fitfully, a human voice imitates the plaintive cry of the peewit, cautious whistling follows, comes next the clash of arms, and the scream of one in the death-throes, and again silence falls. Stroke emerges near the Reekie Broth Pot, wiping his sword and muttering, "Faugh! it drippeth!" At the same moment the air is filled with music of more than mortal — well, the air is filled with music. It seems to come from but a few yards away, and pressing his hand to his throbbing brow the Chevalier presses forward till, pushing aside the branches of a fallen fir, he comes suddenly upon a scene of such romantic beauty that he stands rooted to the ground. Before him, softly lit by a half-moon (the man in it perspiring with curiosity), is a miniature dell, behind which rise threatening rocks, overgrown here and there by grass, heath, and bracken, while in the centre of the dell is a bubbling spring called the Cuttle Well, whose water, as it overflows a natural basin, soaks into the surrounding ground and so finds a way into the picturesque stream below. But it is not the loveliness of the spot which fascinates the prince; rather is it the exquisite creature who sits by the bubbling spring, a reed from a hand-loom in her hands, from which she strikes mournful sounds, 'the while she raises her voice in song. A pink scarf and a blue ribbon are crossed upon her breast, her dark tresses kiss her lovely neck, and as she sits on the only dry stone, her face raised as if in rapt communion with the heavens, and her feet tucked beneath her to avoid the mud, she seems not a human being, but the very spirit of the place and hour. The royal wanderer remains spellbound, while she strikes her lyre and sings (with but one trivial alteration) the song of MacMurrough : —

Awake on your hills, on your islands awake,
Brave sons of the mountains, the frith and the lake!
'Tis the bugle — but not for the chase is the call;
'Tis the pibroch's shrill summons — but not to the hall.

'Tis the summons of heroes for conquest or death,
When the banners are blazing on mountain and heath;
They call to the dirk, the claymore and the targe,
To the march and the muster, the line and the charge.

Be the brand of each Chieftain like Stroke's in his ire!
May the blood through his veins flow like currents of fire!
Burst the base foreign yoke as your sires did of yore,
Or die like your sires, and endure it no more.

As the fair singer concluded, Stroke, who had been deeply moved, heaved a great sigh, and immediately, as if in echo of it, came a sigh from the opposite side of the dell. In a second of time three people had learned that a certain lady had two lovers. She starts to her feet, still carefully avoiding the puddles, but it is not she who speaks.

("Did you hear me?")

("Ay.")

("You're ready?")

("Ca' awa'.")

Stroke dashes to the girl's side, just in time to pluck her from the arms of a masked man. The villain raises his mask and reveals the face of—it looks like Corp, but the disguise is thrown away on Stroke.

"Ha, Cathro," he exclaims joyfully, "so at last we meet on equal terms!"

"Back, Stroke, and let me pass."

"Nay, we fight for the wench."

"So be it. The prideful onion is his who wins her."

"Have at thee, caitiff!"

A terrible conflict ensues. Cathro draws first blood. 'Tis but a scratch. Ha! well thrust, Stroke. In vain Cathro girns his teeth. Inch by inch he is driven back, he slips, he recovers, he pants, he is apparently about to fling himself down the steep bank and so find safety in flight, but he comes on again.

("What are you doing? You run now.")

("I ken, but I'm sweer!")

("Off you go.")

Even as Stroke is about to press home, the cowardly foe flings himself down the steep bank and rolls out of sight. He will give no more trouble to-night; and the victor turns to the Lady Grizel, who had been repinning the silk scarf across her breast, while the issue of the combat was still in doubt.

("Now, then, Grizel, you kiss my hand.")

("I tell you I won't.")

("Well, then, go on your knees to me.")

("You needn't think it.")

("Dagon you! Then ca' awa' standing.")

"My liege, thou hast saved me from the wretch Cathro."

"May I always be near to defend thee in time of danger, my pretty chick."

("Tommy, you promised not to call me by those silly names.")

("They slip out, I tell you. That was aye the way wi' the Stuarts.")

("Well, you must say 'Lady Grizel.') Good, my prince, how can I thank thee?"

"By being my wife. (Not a word of this to Elspeth.)"

"Nay, I summoned thee here to tell thee that can never be. The Grizels of Grizel are of ancient lineage, but they mate not with monarchs. My sire, the nunnery gates will soon close on me forever."

"Then at least say thou lovest me."

"Alas, I love thee not."

("What haver is this? I telled you to say 'Charles, would that I loved thee less.'")

("And I told you I would not.")

("Well, then, where are we now?")

("We miss out all that about my wearing your portrait next my heart, and put in the rich apparel bit, the same as last week.")

("Oh! Then I go on?) Bethink thee, fair jade —"

("Lady.")

"Bethink thee, fair lady, Stuart is not so poor but that, if thou come with him to his lowly lair, he can deck thee with rich apparel and ribbons rare."

" I spurn thy gifts, unhappy man, but if there are holes in —— "

(" Miss that common bit out. I canna thole it.")

(" I like it.) If there are holes in the garments of thy loyal followers, I will come and mend them, and I have a needle and thread in my pocket. (Tommy, there is another button off your shirt! Have you got the button ? ")

"(It's down my breeks.) So be it, proud girl, come ! "

It was Grizel who made masks out of tin rags, picked up where tinkers had passed the night, and musical instruments out of broken reeds that smelled of caddis, and Jacobite head-gear out of weavers' night-caps ; and she kept the lair so clean and tidy as to raise a fear that intruders might mistake its character. Elspeth had to mind the pot, which Aaron Latta never missed, and Corp was supposed to light the fire by striking sparks from his knife, a trick which Tommy considered so easy that he refused to show how it was done. Many strange sauces were boiled in that pot, a sort of potato-turnip pudding often coming out even when not expected, but there was an occasional rabbit that had been bowled over by Corp's unerring hand, and once Tommy shot a — a haunch of venison, having first, with Corp's help, howked it out of Runny-On's swine, then suspended head downward, and open like a book at the page of contents, steaming, dripping, a tub beneath, boys with bladders in the distance. When they had supped they gathered round the fire, Grizel knitting a shawl for they knew whom, but the name was never mentioned, and Tommy told the story of his life at the French court, and how he fought in the '45 and afterwards hid in caves, and so did he shudder, as he described the cold of his bracken beds, and so glowed his face, for it was all real to him, that Grizel let the wool drop on her knee, and Corp whispered to Elspeth, " Dinna be fleid for him; I'se uphaud he found a wy." Those quiet evenings were not the least pleasant spent in the Den.

But sometimes they were interrupted by a fierce endeavour to carry the lair, when boys from Cathro's climbed to it up each other's backs, the rope, of course, having been pulled into safety at the first sound, and then that end of the Den rang with shouts, and deeds of valour on both sides were as common as pine needles, and once Tommy and Corp were only saved from captors who had them down, by Grizel rushing into the midst of things with two flaring torches, and another time bold Birkie, most daring of the storming party, was seized with two others and made to walk the plank. The plank had been part of a gate, and was suspended over the bank of the Silent Pool, so that, as you approached the farther end, down you went. It was not a Jacobite method, but Tommy feared that rows of bodies, hanging from the trees still standing in the Den, might attract attention.

CHAPTER XXIII

LESS alarming but more irritating was the attempt of the youth of Monypenny and the West town end, to establish a rival firm of Jacobites (without even being sure of the name). They started business (Francie Crabb leader, because he had a kilt) on a flagon of porter and an ounce of twist, which they carried on a stick through the Den, saying "Bowf!" like dogs, when they met anyone, and then laughing doubtfully. The twist and porter were seized by Tommy and his followers, and Haggerty-Taggerty, Major, arrived home with his head so firmly secured in the flagon that the solder had to be melted before he saw the world again. Francie was in still worse plight, for during the remainder of the evening he had to hide in shame among the brackens, and Tommy wore a kilt.

One cruel revenge the beaten rivals had. They waylaid Grizel, when she was alone, and thus assailed her, she answering not a word.

" What's a father ? "

"She'll soon no have a mither either!"

" The Painted Lady needs to paint her cheeks no longer ! ' "

" Na, the red spots comes themsels now."

" Have you heard her hoasting ? "

" Ay, it's the hoast o' a dying woman."

" The joiner heard it, and gave her a look, measuring her wi' his eye for the coffin. 'Five and a half by one and a half would hold her snod,' he says to himsel'."

" Ronny-On's auld wife heard it, and says she, 'Dinna think, my leddy, as you'll be buried in consecrated ground.' "

" Na, a'body kens she'll just be hauled at the end o' a rope to the hole where the witches was shooled in."

" Wi' a paling spar through her, to keep her down on the day o' judgment."

Well, well, these children became men and women in time, one of them even a bit of a hero, though he never knew it.

Are you angry with them ?   If so, put the cheap thing aside, or think only of Grizel, and perhaps God will turn your anger into love for her.

Great-hearted, solitary child ! She walked away from them without flinching, but on reaching the Den, where no one could see her — she lay down on the ground, and her cheeks were dry, but little wells of water stood in her eyes.

She would not be the Lady Grizel that night.

She went home instead, but there was something she wanted to ask Tommy now, and the next time she saw him she began at once. Grizel always began at once, often in the middle, she saw what she was making for so clearly.

"Do you know what it means when there are red spots in your cheeks, that used not to be there?"

Tommy knew at once to whom she was referring, for he had heard the gossip of the youth of Monypenny, and he hesitated to answer.

"And if, when you cough, you bring up a tiny speck of blood?"

"I would get a bottle frae the doctor," said Tommy, evasively.

"She won't have the doctor," answered Grizel, unguardedly, and then with a look dared Tommy to say that she spoke of her mother.

"Does it mean you are dying?"

"I — I — oh, no, they soon get better."

He said this because he was so sorry for Grizel. There never was a more sympathetic nature than Tommy's. At every time of his life his pity was easily roused for persons in distress, and he sought to comfort them by shutting their eyes to the truth as long as possible. This sometimes brought relief to them, but it was useless to Grizel, who must face her troubles.

"Why don't you answer truthfully?" she cried, with vehemence. "It is so easy to be truthful!"

294

" Well, then," said Tommy, reluctantly, " I think they generally die."

Elspeth often carried in her pocket a little Testament, presented to her by the Rev. Mr. Dishart for learning by heart one of the noblest of books, the Shorter Catechism, as Scottish children do or did, not understanding it at the time, but its meaning comes long afterwards and suddenly, when you have most need of it. Sometimes Elspeth read aloud from her Testament to Grizel, who made no comment, but this same evening, when the two were alone, she said abruptly:

" Have you your Testament ? "

" Yes," Elspeth said, producing it.

" Which is the page about saving sinners ? "

" It's all about that."

" But the page when you are in a hurry ? "

Elspeth read aloud the story of the Crucifixion, and Grizel listened sharply until she heard what Jesus said to the malefactor : " To-day shalt thou be with me in Paradise."

" And was he ? "

" Of course."

" But he had been wicked all his life, and I believe he was only good, just that minute, because they were crucifying him. If they had let him come down —— "

" No, he repented, you know. That means he had faith, and if you have faith you are saved. It doesna matter how bad you have been. You have just to say ' I believe' before you die, and God lets you in. It's so easy, Grizel," cried Elspeth, with shining eyes.

Grizel pondered. "I don't believe it is so easy as that," she said, decisively.

Nevertheless she asked presently what the Testament cost, and when Elspeth answered "Fourpence," offered her the money.

" I don't want to sell it," Elspeth remonstrated.

" If you don't give it to me, I shall take it from you," said Grizel, determinedly.

" You can buy one."

" No, the shop people would guess."

" Guess what ? "

" I won't tell you."

" I'll lend it to you."

" I won't take it that way." So Elspeth had to part with her Testament, saying wonderingly, "Can you read ? "

" Yes, and write too. Mamma taught me."

" But I thought she was daft," Elspeth blurted out.

" She is only daft now and then," Grizel replied, without her usual spirit. "Generally she is not daft at all, but only timid."

Next morning the Painted Lady's child paid three calls, one in town, two in the country. The adorable thing is that, once having made up her mind, she never flinched, not even when her hand was on the knocker.

The first gentleman received her in his lobby. For a moment he did not remember her; then suddenly the colour deepened on his face, and he went back and shut the parlour-door.

" Did anybody see you coming here ? " he asked, quickly.

" I don't know."

" What does she want ? "

" She did not send me, I came myself."

" Well ? "

" When you come to our house —— "

" I never come to your house."

" That is a lie."

" Speak lower ! "

" When you come to our house you tell me to go out and play. But I don't. I go and cry."

No doubt he was listening, but his eyes were on the parlour-door.

" I don't know why I cry, but you know, you wicked man ! Why is it ?

" Why is it ? " she demanded again, like a queen-child, but he could only fidget with his gold chain and shuffle uneasily in his parnella shoes.

" You are not coming to see my mamma again."

The gentleman gave her an ugly look.

" If you do," she said at once, " I shall come

straight here and open that door you are looking at, and tell your wife."

He dared not swear. His hand ——

"If you offer me money," said Grizel, "I shall tell her now."

He muttered something to himself.

"Is it true?" she asked, "that mamma is dying?"

This was a genuine shock to him, for he had not been at Double Dykes since winter, and then the Painted Lady was quite well.

"Nonsense!" he said, and his obvious disbelief brought some comfort to the girl. But she asked, "Why are there red spots on her cheeks, then?"

"Paint," he answered.

"No," cried Grizel, rocking her arms, "it is not paint now. I thought it might be and I tried to rub it off while she was sleeping, but it will not come off. And when she coughs there is blood on her handkerchief."

He looked alarmed now, and Grizel's fears came back. "If mamma dies," she said determinedly, "she must be buried in the cemetery."

"She is not dying, I tell you."

"And you must come to the funeral."

"Are you gyte?"

"With crape on your hat."

His mouth formed an emphatic "No."

"You must," said Grizel, firmly, "you shall!

298

If you don't ——" She pointed to the parlour-door.

Her remaining two visits were to a similar effect, and one of the gentlemen came out of the ordeal somewhat less shamefully than the first, the other worse, for he blubbered and wanted to kiss her. It is questionable whether many young ladies have made such a profound impression in a series of morning calls.

The names of these gentlemen are not known, but you shall be told presently where they may be found. Every person in Thrums used to know the place, and many itched to get at the names, but as yet no one has had the nerve to look for them.

Not at this time did Grizel say a word of these interviews to her friends, though Tommy had to be told of them later, and she never again referred to her mother at the Saturday evenings in the Den. But the others began to know a queer thing, nothing less than this, that in their absence the lair was sometimes visited by a person or persons unknown, who made use of their stock of firewood. It was a startling discovery, but when they discussed it in council, Grizel never contributed a word. The affair remained a mystery until one Saturday evening, when Tommy and Elspeth, reaching the lair first, found in it a delicate white shawl. They both recognized in it the pretty thing the Painted

Lady had pinned across her shoulders on the night they saw her steal out of Double Dykes to meet the man of long ago.

Even while their eyes were saying this, Grizel climbed in without giving the password, and they knew from her quick glance around that she had come for the shawl. She snatched it out of Tommy's hand with a look that prohibited questions.

" It's the pair o' them," Tommy said to Elspeth at the first opportunity, "that sometimes comes here at nights and kindles the fire and warms themsels at the gloze. And the last time they came they forgot the shawl."

" I dinna like to think the Painted Lady has been up here, Tommy."

" But she has. You ken how, when she has a daft fit, she wanders the Den trysting the man that never comes. Has she no been seen at all hours o' the night, Grizel following a wee bit ahint, like as if to take tent o' her ? "

" They say that, and that Grizel canna get her to go home till the daft fit has passed."

" Well, she has that kechering hoast and spit now, and so Grizel brings her up here out o' the blasts."

" But how could she be got to come here, if she winna go home ? "

" Because frae here she can watch for the man."

Elspeth shuddered. "Do you think she's here often, Tommy?" she asked.

"Just when she has a daft fit on, and they say she's wise sax days in seven."

This made the Jacobite meetings eerie events for Elspeth, but Tommy liked them the better; and what were they not to Grizel, who ran to them with passionate fondness every Saturday night? Sometimes she even outdistanced her haunting dreads, for she knew that her mother did not think herself seriously ill; and had not the three gentlemen made light of that curious cough? So there were nights when the lair saw Grizel go riotous with glee, laughing, dancing, and shouting overmuch, like one trying to make up for a lost childhood. But it was also noticed that when the time came to leave the Den she was very loath, and kissed her hands to the places where she had been happiest, saying, wistfully, and with pretty gestures that were foreign to Thrums, "Good-night, dear Cuttle Well!" "Good-by, sweet, sweet Lair!" as if she knew it could not last. These weekly risings in the Den were most real to Tommy, but it was Grizel who loved them best.

CHAPTER XXIV

A ROMANCE OF TWO OLD MAIDS AND A STOUT BACHELOR

CAME Gavinia, a burgess of the besieged city, along the south shore of the Silent Pool. She was but a maid seeking to know what love might be, and as she wandered on, she nibbled dreamily at a hot sweet-smelling bridie, whose gravy oozed deliciously through a bursting paper-bag.

It was a fit night for dark deeds.

"Methinks she cometh to her doom!"

The speaker was a masked man who had followed her — he was sniffing ecstatically — since she left the city walls.

She seemed to possess a charmed life. He would have had her in Shovel Gorge, but just then Ronny-On's Jean and Peter Scrymgeour turned the corner.

Suddenly Gavinia felt an exquisite thrill: a man was pursuing her. She slipped the paper-bag out of sight, holding it dexterously against her side with her arm, so that the gravy should not spurt out, and ran. Lights flashed, a kingly voice cried "Now!" and immediately a petticoat was flung over her head. (The Lady Griselda looked thin that evening.)

Gavinia was dragged to the Lair, and though many a time they bumped her, she tenderly nursed the paper-bag with her arm, or fondly thought she did so, for when unmuffled she discovered that it had been removed, as if by painless surgery. And her captors' tongues were sweeping their chins for stray crumbs.

The wench was offered her choice of Stroke's gallant fellows, but "Wha carries me wears me," said she, promptly, and not only had he to carry her from one end of the Den to the other, but he must do it whistling, as if barely conscious that she was there. So after many attempts (for she was always willing to let them have their try) Corp of Corp, speaking for Sir Joseph and the others, announced a general retreat.

Instead of taking this prisoner's life, Stroke made her his tool, releasing her on condition that every seventh day she appeared at the Lair with information concerning the doings in the town. Also, her name was Agnes of Kingoldrum, and, if she said it was not, the plank. Bought thus, Agnes proved of service, bringing such bags of news that Stroke was often occupied now in drawing diagrams of Thrums and its strongholds, including the residence of Cathro, with dotted lines to show the direction of proposed underground passages.

And presently came by this messenger disquieting rumours indeed. Another letter, being the third in six months, had reached the Dovecot, addressed, not to Miss Ailie, but to Miss Kitty. Miss Kitty had been dead fully six years, and Archie Piatt, the post, swore that this was the eighteenth, if not the nineteenth, letter he had delivered to her name since that time. They were all in the same hand, a man's, and there had been similar letters while she was alive, but of these he kept no record. Miss Ailie always took these letters with a trembling hand, and then locked herself in her bedroom, leaving the key in such a position in its hole that you might just as well go straight back to the kitchen. Within a few hours of the arrival of these ghostly letters, tongues were wagging about them, but to the two or three persons who (after passing a sleepless night) bluntly asked Miss Ailie from whom they came, she only replied by pursing her lips. Nothing could be learned at the post-office save that Miss Ailie never posted any letter there, except to two Misses and a Mrs., all resident in Redlintie. The mysterious letters came from Australy or Manchester, or some such part.

What could Stroke make of this? He expressed no opinion, but oh, his face was grim. Orders were immediately given to double the sentinels. A barrel was placed in the Queen's Bower. Sawdust was introduced at immense risk into the Lair.

A paper containing this writing, " 248xho317 Oxh-4591AWS314 14dd5," was passed round and then solemnly burned. Nothing was left to chance.

Agnes of Kingoldrum (Stroke told her) did not know Miss Ailie, but she was commanded to pay special attention to the gossip of the town regarding this new move of the enemy. By next Saturday the plot had thickened. Previous letters might have reddened Miss Ailie's eyes for an hour or two, but they gladdened her as a whole. Now she sat crying all evening with this one on her lap; she gave up her daily walk to the Berlin wool shop, with all its romantic possibilities; at the clatter of the tea-things she would start apprehensively; she had let a red shawl lie for two days in the blue-and-white room.

Stroke never blanched. He called his faithful remnant around him, and told them the story of Bell the Cat, with its application in the records of his race. Did they take his meaning? This Miss Ailie must be watched closely. In short, once more, in Scottish history, someone must bell the cat. Who would volunteer?

Corp of Corp and Sir Joseph stepped forward as one man.

" Thou couldst not look like Gavinia," the prince said, shaking his head.

" Wha wants him to look like Gavinia ? " cried an indignant voice.

"Peace, Agnes!" said Stroke.

"Agnes, why bletherest thou?" said Sir Joseph.

"If onybody's to watch Miss Ailie," insisted the obstinate woman, "surely it should be me!"

"Ha!" Stroke sprang to his feet, for something in her voice, or the outline of her figure, or perhaps it was her profile, had given him an idea. "A torch!" he cried eagerly, and with its aid he scanned her face until his own shone triumphant.

"He kens a wy, methinks!" exclaimed one of his men.

Sir Joseph was right. It had been among the prince's exploits to make his way into Thrums in disguise, and mix with the people as one of themselves, and on several of these occasions he had seen Miss Ailie's attendant. Agnes's resemblance to her now struck him for the first time. It should be Agnes of Kingoldrum's honourable though dangerous part to take this Gavinia's place.

But how to obtain possession of Gavinia's person? Agnes made several suggestions, but was told to hold her prating peace. It could only be done in one way. They must kidnap her. Sir Joseph was ordered to be ready to accompany his liege on this perilous enterprise in ten minutes. "And mind," said Stroke, gravely, "we carry our lives in our hands."

"In our hands!" gasped Sir Joseph, greatly

puzzled, but he dared ask no more, and when the two set forth (leaving Agnes of Kingoldrum looking very uncomfortable), he was surprised to see that Stroke was carrying nothing. Sir Joseph carried in his hand his red hanky, mysteriously knotted.

" Where is yours ? " he whispered.

" What meanest thou ? "

Sir Joseph replied, " Oh, nothing," and thought it best to slip his handkerchief into his trouser-pocket, but the affair bothered him for long afterwards.

When they returned through the Den, there still seemed (to the unpiercing eye) to be but two of them ; nevertheless, Stroke reëntered the Lair to announce to Agnes and the others that he had left Gavinia below in charge of Sir Joseph. She was to walk the plank anon, but first she must be stripped that Agnes might don her garments. Stroke was every inch a prince, so he kept Agnes by his side, and sent down the Lady Griselda and Widow Elspeth to strip the prisoner, Sir Joseph having orders to stand back fifty paces. (It is a pleasure to have to record this.)

The signal having been given that this delicate task was accomplished, Stroke whistled shrilly, and next moment was heard from far below a thud, as of a body falling in water, then an agonizing shriek, and then again all was still, save for the heavy breathing of Agnes of Kingoldrum.

Sir Joseph (very wet) returned to the Lair, and Agnes was commanded to take off her clothes in a retired spot and put on those of the deceased which she should find behind a fallen tree.

"I winna be called the deceased," cried Agnes hotly, but she had to do as she was bid, and when she emerged from behind the tree she was the very image of the ill-fated Gavinia. Stroke showed her a plan of Miss Ailie's backdoor, and also gave her a kitchen key (when he produced this, she felt in her pockets and then snatched it from him), after which she set out for the Dovecot in a scare about her own identity.

"And now, what doest thou think about it a'?" inquired Sir Joseph eagerly, to which Stroke made answer, looking at him fixedly:

"The wind is in the west!"

Sir Joseph should have kept this a secret, but soon Stroke heard Inverquharity prating of it, and he called his lieutenant before him. Sir Joseph acknowledged humbly that he had been unable to hide it from Inverquharity, but he promised not to tell Muckle Kenny, of whose loyalty there were doubts. Henceforth, when the faithful fellow was Muckle Kenny, he would say doggedly to himself, "Dinna question me, Kenny. I ken nocht about it."

Dark indeed were now the fortunes of the Pretender, but they had one bright spot. Miss Ailie had been taken in completely by the trick played on her, and thus Stroke now got full information of the enemy's doings. Cathro having failed to dislodge the Jacobites, the seat of war had been changed by Victoria to the Dovecot, whither her despatches were now forwarded. That this last one, of which Agnes of Kingoldrum tried in vain to obtain possession, doubled the price on the Pretender's head, there could be no doubt; but as Miss Ailie was a notorious Hanoverian, only the hunted prince himself knew why this should make her cry.

He hinted with a snigger something about an affair he had once had with the lady.

The Widow and Sir Joseph accepted this explanation, but it made Lady Griselda rock her arms in irritation.

The reports about Miss Ailie's behaviour became more and more alarming. She walked up and down her bed-room now in the middle of the night. Every time the knocker clanked she held herself together with both hands. Agnes had orders not to answer the door until her mistress had keeked through the window.

"She's expecting a veesitor, methinks," said Corp. This was his bright day.

"Ay," answered Agnes, "but is't a man-body, or just a woman-body?"

Leaving the rebels in the Lair stunned by Victoria's latest move, we now return to Thrums, where Miss Ailie's excited state had indeed been the talk of many. Even the gossips, however, had underestimated her distress of mind, almost as much as they misunderstood its cause. You must listen now (will you?) to so mild a thing as the long thin romance of two maiden ladies and a stout bachelor, all beginning to be old the day the three of them first drank tea together, and that was ten years ago.

Miss Ailie and Miss Kitty, you may remember, were not natives of Thrums. They had been born and brought up at Redlintie, and on the death of their parents they had remained there, the gauger having left them all his money, which was just sufficient to enable them to live like ladies, if they took tiny Magenta Cottage, and preferred an inexperienced maid. At first their life was very quiet, the walk from eleven to one for the good of fragile Miss Kitty's health its outstanding feature. When they strolled together on the cliffs, Miss Ailie's short thick figure, straight as an elvint, cut the wind in two, but Miss Kitty was swayed this way and that, and when she shook her curls at the wind, it blew them roguishly in her face, and had another shot at them, as soon as they were put to rights. If the two walked by the shore (where the younger sometimes bathed her feet, the elder keeping a sharp eye on land and water), the sea behaved like the wind, dodging Miss Ailie's ankles and snapping playfully at Miss Kitty's. Thus even the elements could distinguish between the sisters, who nevertheless had so much in common that at times Miss Ailie would look into her mirror and sigh to think that some day Miss Kitty might be like this. How Miss Ailie adored Miss Kitty! She trembled with pleasure if you said Miss Kitty was pretty, and she dreamed dreams in which she herself walked as bridesmaid only. And just as Miss Ailie could be romantic, Miss Kitty, the romantic, could be prim, and the primness was her own as much as the curls, but Miss Ailie usually carried it for her, like a cloak in case of rain.

Not often have two sweeter women grown together on one stem. What were the men of Redlintie about? The sisters never asked each other this question, but there were times when, apparently without cause, Miss Ailie hugged Miss Kitty vehemently, as if challenging the world, and perhaps Miss Kitty understood.

Thus a year or more passed uneventfully, until the one romance of their lives befell them. It began with the reappearance in Redlintie of Magerful Tam, who had come to torment his father into giving him more money, but, finding he had come too late, did not harass the sisters. This is perhaps the best thing that can be told of him, and, as if he knew this, he had often told it himself to Jean

Myles, without however telling her what followed. For something to his advantage did follow, and it was greatly to the credit of Miss Ailie and Miss Kitty, though they went about it as timidly as if they were participating in a crime. Ever since they learned of the sin which had brought this man into the world their lives had been saddened, for on the same day they realized what a secret sorrow had long lain at their mother's heart. Alison Sibbald was a very simple gracious lady, who never recovered from the shock of discovering that she had married a libertine; yet she had pressed her husband to do something for his son, and been greatly pained when he refused with a coarse laugh. The daughters were very like her in nature, and though the knowledge of what she had suffered increased many fold their love for her, so that in her last days their passionate devotion to her was the talk of Redlintie, it did not blind them to what seemed to them to be their duty to the man. As their father's son, they held, he had a right to a third of the gauger's money, and to withhold it from him, now that they knew his whereabouts, would have been a form of theft. But how to give T. his third? They called him T. from delicacy, and they had never spoken to him. When he passed them in the streets, they turned pale, and, thinking of their mother, looked another way. But they knew he winked.

At last, looking red in one street, and white in another, but resolute in all, they took their business to the office of Mr. John McLean, the writer, who had once escorted Miss Kitty home from a party without anything coming of it, so that it was quite a psychological novel in several volumes. Now Mr. John happened to be away at the fishing, and a reckless maid showed them into the presence of a strange man, who was no other than his brother Ivie, home for a year's holiday from India, and naturally this extraordinary occurrence so agitated them that Miss Ailie had told half her story before she realized that Miss Kitty was titting at her dress. Then indeed she sought to withdraw, but Ivie, with the alarming yet not unpleasing audacity of his sex, said he had heard enough to convince him that in this matter he was qualified to take his brother's place. But he was not, for he announced, " My advice to you is not to give T. a halfpenny," which showed that he did not even understand what they had come about.

They begged permission to talk to each other behind the door, and presently returned, troubled but brave. Miss Kitty whispered " Courage!" and this helped Miss Ailie to the deed.

" We have quite made up our minds to let T. have the money," she said, " but—but the difficulty is the taking it to him. Must we take it in person ? "

"Why not?" asked Ivie, bewildered.

"It would be such a painful meeting to us," said Miss Ailie.

"And to him," added simple Miss Kitty.

"You see we have thought it best not to—not to know him," said Miss Ailie, faintly.

"Mother—" faltered Miss Kitty, and at the word the eyes of both ladies began to fill.

Then, of course, Mr. McLean discovered the object of their visit, and promised that his brother should take this delicate task off their hands, and as he bowed them out he said, "Ladies, I think you are doing a very foolish thing, and I shall respect you for it all my life." At least Miss Kitty insisted that respect was the word, Miss Ailie thought he said esteem.

That was how it began, and it progressed for nearly a year at a rate that will take away your breath. On the very next day he met Miss Kitty in High Street, a most awkward encounter for her ("for, you know, Ailie, we were never introduced, so how could I decide all in a moment what to do?"), and he raised his hat (the Misses Croall were at their window and saw the whole thing). But we must gallop, like the friendship. He bowed the first two times, the third time he shook hands (by a sort of providence Miss Kitty had put on her new mittens), the fourth, fifth, and sixth times he conversed, the seventh time he—they replied that they could really not trouble him so much, but he said he was going that way at any rate; the eighth time, ninth time, and tenth times the figures of two ladies and a gentleman might have been observed, etc., and either the eleventh or twelfth time ("Fancy our not being sure, Ailie" — "It has all come so quickly, Kitty") he took his first dish of tea at Magenta Cottage.

There were many more walks after this, often along the cliffs to a little fishing village, over which the greatest of magicians once stretched his wand, so that it became famous forever, as all the world saw except himself; and tea at the cottage followed, when Ivie asked Miss Kitty to sing "The Land o' the Leal," and Miss Ailie sat by the window, taking in her merino, that it might fit Miss Kitty, cutting her sable muff (once Alison Sibbald's) into wristbands for Miss Kitty's astrakhan; they did not go quite all the way round, but men are blind.

Ivie was not altogether blind. The sisters, it is to be feared, called him the dashing McLean, but he was at this time nearly forty years old, an age when bachelors like to take a long rest from thinking of matrimony, before beginning again. Fifteen years earlier he had been in love, but the girl had not cared to wait for him, and though in India he had often pictured himself returning to Redlintie to gaze wistfully at her old home, when he did come back he never went, because the house was a little out of the way. But unknown to him two ladies went, to whom he had told this as a rather dreary joke. They were ladies he esteemed very much, though having a sense of humour he sometimes chuckled on his way home from Magenta Cottage, and he thought out many ways of adding little pleasures to their lives. It was like him to ask Miss Kitty to sing and play, though he disliked music. He understood that it is a hard world for single women, and knew himself for a very ordinary sort of man. If it ever crossed his head that Miss Kitty would be willing to marry him, he felt genuinely sorry at the same time that she had not done better long ago. He never flattered himself that he could be accepted now, save for the good home he could provide (he was not the man to blame women for being influenced by that), for like most of his sex he was unaware that a woman is never too old to love or to be loved; if they do know it, the mean ones among them make a jest of it, at which (God knows why) their wives laugh. Mr. McLean had been acquainted with the sisters for months before he was sure even that Miss Kitty was his favourite. He found that out one evening when sitting with an old friend, whose wife and children were in the room, gathered round a lamp and playing at some child's game. Suddenly Ivie McLean envied his friend, and at the same moment he thought tenderly of Miss Kitty. But the feeling passed. He experienced it next and as suddenly when arriving at Bombay, where some women were waiting to greet their husbands.

Before he went away the two gentlewomen knew that he was not to speak. They did not tell each other what was in their minds. Miss Kitty was so bright during those last days, that she must have deceived anyone who did not love her, and Miss Ailie held her mouth very tight, and if possible was straighter than ever, but oh, how gentle she was with Miss Kitty! Ivie's last two weeks in the old country were spent in London, and during that time Miss Kitty liked to go away by herself, and sit on a rock and gaze at the sea. Once Miss Ailie followed her and would have called him a ——

"Don't, Ailie!" said Miss Kitty, imploringly. But that night, when Miss Kitty was brushing her hair, she said courageously, "Ailie, I don't think I should wear curls any longer. You know I—I shall be thirty-seven in August." And after the elder sister had become calm again, Miss Kitty said timidly, "You don't think I have been unladylike, do you, Ailie?"

Such a trifle now remains to tell. Miss Kitty was the better business woman of the two, and kept the accounts, and understood, as Miss Ailie could not understand, how their little income was invested, and even knew what consols were, though never quite certain whether it was their fall or rise that is matter for congratulation. And after the ship had sailed, she told Miss Ailie that nearly all their money was lost, and that she had known it for a month.

"And you kept it from me! Why?"

"I thought, Ailie, that you, knowing I am not strong—that you—would perhaps tell him."

"And I would!" cried Miss Ailie.

"And then," said Miss Kitty, "perhaps he, out of pity, you know!"

"Well, even if he had!" said Miss Ailie.

"I could not, oh, I could not," replied Miss Kitty, flushing; "it—it would not have been ladylike, Ailie."

Thus forced to support themselves, the sisters decided to keep school genteelly, and, hearing that there was an opening in Thrums, they settled there, and Miss Kitty brushed her hair out now, and with a twist and a twirl ran it up her fingers into a net, whence by noon some of it had escaped through the little windows and was curls again. She and Miss Ailie were happy in Thrums, for time took the pain out of the affair of Mr. Mc-Lean, until it became not merely a romantic memory, but, with the letters he wrote to Miss Kitty and her answers, the great quiet pleasure of their lives. They were friendly letters only, but Miss Kitty wrote hers out in pencil first and read them to Miss Ailie, who had been taking notes for them.

In the last weeks of Miss Kitty's life Miss Ailie conceived a passionate unspoken hatred of Mr. McLean, and her intention was to write and tell him that he had killed her darling. But owing to the illness into which she was flung by Miss Kitty's death, that unjust letter was never written.

But why did Mr. McLean continue to write to Miss Kitty?

Well, have pity or be merciless as you choose. For several years Mr. McLean's letters had been the one thing the sisters looked forward to, and now, when Miss Ailie was without Miss Kitty, must she lose them also? She never doubted, though she may have been wrong, that, if Ivie knew of Miss Kitty's death, one letter would come in answer, and that the last. She could not tell him. In the meantime he wrote twice asking the reason of this long silence, and at last Miss Ailie, whose handwriting was very like her sister's, wrote him a letter which was posted at Tilliedrum and signed " Katherine Cray." The thing seems monstrous, but this gentle lady did it, and it was never so difficult to do again. Latterly, it had been easy.

This last letter of Mr. McLean's announced to Miss Kitty that he was about to start for home " for good," and he spoke in it of coming to

Thrums to see the sisters, as soon as he reached Redlintie. Poor Miss Ailie! After sleepless nights she trudged to the Tilliedrum post-office with a full confession of her crime, which would be her welcome home to him when he arrived at his brother's house. Many of the words were written on damp blobs. After that she could do nothing but wait for the storm, and waiting she became so meek, that Gavinia, who loved her because she was " that simple," said sorrowfully:

" How is't you never rage at me now, ma'am? I'm sure it keepit you lightsome, and I likit to hear the bum o't."

" And instead o' the raging I was prigging for," the soft-hearted maid told her friends, " she gave me a flannel petticoat!" Indeed, Miss Ailie had taken to giving away her possessions at this time, like a woman who thought she was on her death-bed. There was something for each of her pupils, including — but the important thing is that there was a gift for Tommy, which had the effect of planting the Hanoverian Woman (to whom he must have given many uneasy moments) more securely on the British Throne.

CHAPTER XXV

A PENNY PASS-BOOK

Elspeth conveyed the gift to Tommy in a brown paper wrapping, and when it lay revealed as an aging volume of *Mamma's Boy*, a magazine for the Home, nothing could have looked more harmless. But, ah, you never know. Hungrily Tommy ran his eye through the bill of fare for something choice to begin with, and he found it. " The Boy Pirate " it was called. Never could have been fairer promise, and down he sat confidently.

It was a paper on the boys who have been undone by reading pernicious fiction. It gave their names, and the number of pistols they had bought, and what the judge said when he pronounced sentence. It counted the sensational tales found beneath the bed, and described the desolation of the mothers and sisters. It told the colour of the father's hair before and afterwards.

Tommy flung the thing from him, picked it up again, and read on uneasily, and when at last he rose he was shrinking from himself. In hopes that he might sleep it off he went early to bed, but his contrition was still with him in the morning. Then Elspeth was shown the article which had saved him, and she, too, shuddered at what she had been, though her remorse was but a poor display beside his, he was so much better at everything than Elspeth. Tommy's distress of mind was so genuine and so keen that it had several hours' start of his admiration of it; and it was still sincere, though he himself had become gloomy, when he told his followers that they were no more. Grizel heard his tale with disdain, and said she hated Miss Ailie for giving him the silly book, but he reproved these unchristian sentiments, while admitting that Miss Ailie had played on him a scurvy trick.

"But you're glad you've repented, Tommy," Elspeth reminded him, anxiously.

"Ay, I'm glad," he answered, without heartiness.

"Well, gin you repent I'll repent too," said Corp, always ready to accept Tommy without question.

"You'll be happier," replied Tommy, sourly.

"Ay, to be good's the great thing," Corp growled; "but, Tommy, could we no have just one michty blatter, methinks, to end up wi'?"

This, of course, could not be, and Saturday forenoon found Tommy wandering the streets listlessly, very happy, you know, but inclined to kick at any one who came near, such, for instance, as the stranger who asked him in the square if he could point out the abode of Miss Ailie Cray.

Tommy led the way, casting some converted looks at the gentleman, and judging him to be the mysterious unknown in whom the late Captain Stroke had taken such a reprehensible interest. He was a stout, red-faced man, stepping firmly into the fifties, with a beard that even the most converted must envy, and a frown sat on his brows all the way, proving him possibly ill-tempered, but also one of the notable few who can think hard about one thing for at least five consecutive minutes. Many took a glint at him as he passed, but missed the frown, they were wondering so much why the fur of his heavy top-coat was on the inside, where it made little show, save at blasty corners.

Miss Ailie was in her parlour, trying to give her mind to a blue and white note-book, but when she saw who was coming up the garden she dropped the little volume and tottered to her bedroom. She was there when Gavinia came up to announce that she had shown a gentleman into the blue-and-white room, who gave the name of Ivie McLean. "Tell him — I shall come down — presently," gasped Miss Ailie, and then Gavinia was sure this was the man who was making her mistress so unhappy.

"She's so easily flichtered now," Gavinia told Tommy in the kitchen, "that for fear o' starting her I never whistle at my work without telling her I'm to do't, and if I fall on the stair, my first thought is to jump up and cry, 'It was just me tum'ling.' And now I believe this brute'll be the death o' her."

"But what can he do to her?"

"I dinna ken, but she's greeting sair, and you can hear how he's rampaging up and down the blue-and-white room. Listen to his thrawn feet! He's raging because she's so long in coming down, and come she daurna. Oh, the poor crittur!"

Now, Tommy was very fond of his old schoolmistress, and he began to be unhappy with Gavinia.

"She hasna a man-body in the world to take care o' her," sobbed the girl.

"Has she no?" cried Tommy, fiercely, and under one of the impulses that so easily mastered him he marched into the blue-and-white room.

"Well, my young friend, and what may you want?" asked Mr. McLean, impatiently.

Tommy sat down and folded his arms. "I'm going to sit here and see what you do to Miss Ailie," he said, determinedly.

Mr. McLean said "Oh!" and then seemed favourably impressed, for he added quietly: "She is a friend of yours, is she? Well, I have no intention of hurting her."

"You had better no," replied Tommy, stoutly.

"Did she send you here?"

324

"No; I came mysel'."

"To protect her?"

There was the irony in it that so puts up a boy's dander. "Dinna think," said Tommy, hotly, "that I'm fleid at you, though I have no beard — at least, I hinna it wi' me."

At this unexpected conclusion a smile crossed Mr. McLean's face, but was gone in an instant. "I wish you had laughed," said Tommy, on the watch; "once a body laughs he canna be angry no more," which was pretty good even for Tommy. It made Mr. McLean ask him why he was so fond of Miss Ailie.

"I'm the only man-body she has," he answered.

"Oh? But why are you her man-body?"

The boy could think of no better reason than this: "Because — because she's so sair in need o' ane." (There were moments when one liked Tommy.)

Mr. McLean turned to the window, and perhaps forgot that he was not alone. "Well, what are you thinking about so deeply?" he asked by and by.

"I was trying to think o' something that would gar you laugh," answered Tommy, very earnestly, and was surprised to see that he had nearly done it.

The blue and white note-book was lying on the floor where Miss Ailie had dropped it. Often in Tommy's presence she had consulted this work, and certainly its effect on her was the reverse of laughter; but once he had seen Dr. McQueen pick it up and roar over every page. With an inspiration Tommy handed the book to Mr. McLean. "It made the doctor laugh," he said persuasively.

"Go away," said Ivie, impatiently; "I am in no mood for laughing."

"I tell you what," answered Tommy, "I'll go, if you promise to look at it," and to be rid of him the man agreed. For the next quarter of an hour Tommy and Gavinia were very near the door of the blue-and-white room, Tommy whispering dejectedly, "I hear no laughing," and Gavinia replying, "But he has quieted down."

Mr. McLean had a right to be very angry, but God only can say whether he had a right to be as angry as he was. The book had been handed to him open, and he was laying it down unread when a word underlined caught his eye. It was his own name. Nothing in all literature arrests our attention quite so much as that. He sat down to the book. It was just about this time that Miss Ailie went on her knees to pray.

It was only a penny pass-book. On its blue cover had been pasted a slip of white paper, and on the paper was written, in blue ink, "Alison Cray," with a date nearly nine years old. The contents were in Miss Ailie's prim handwriting; jottings for her own use begun about the time

326

when the sisters, trembling at their audacity, had opened school, and consulted and added to fitfully ever since. Hours must have been spent in erasing the blots and other blemishes so carefully. The tiny volume was not yet full, and between its two last written pages lay a piece of blue blotting-paper neatly cut to the size of the leaf.

Some of these notes were transcripts from books, some contained the advice of friends, others were doubtless the result of talks with Miss Kitty (from whom there were signs that the work had been kept a secret), many were Miss Ailie's own. An entry of this kind was frequent: " If you are un-certain of the answer to a question in arithmetic, it is advisable to leave the room on some pretext and work out the sum swiftly in the passage." Various pretexts were suggested, and this one (which had an insufficient line through it) had been inserted by Dr. McQueen on that day when Tommy saw him chuckling, " You pretend that your nose is bleeding, and putting your handker-chief to it, retire hastily, the supposition being that you have gone to put the key of the blue-and-white room down your back." Evidently these small deceptions troubled Miss Ailie, for she had written, " Such subterfuge is, I hope, pardonable, the object being the maintenance of scholastic dis-cipline." On another page, where the arithmetic was again troubling her, this appeared: " If Kitty were aware that the squealing of the slate-pencils gave me such headaches, she would insist on again taking the arithmetic class, though it always makes her ill. Surely, then, I am justified in saying that the sound does not distress me." To this the doctor had added, " You are a brick."

There were two pages headed NEVER, which mentioned ten things that Miss Ailie must never do; among them, " *Never* let the big boys know you are afraid of them. To awe them, stamp with the foot, speak in a loud ferocious voice, and look them unflinchingly in the face."

" Punishments " was another heading, but she had written it small, as if to prevent herself seeing it each time she opened the book. Obviously her hope had been to dispose of Punishment in a few lines, but it would have none of that, and Mr. McLean found it stalking from page to page. Miss Ailie favoured the cane in preference to tawse, which " often flap round your neck as you are about to bring them down." Except in desperate cases " it will probably be found sufficient to order the offender to bring the cane to you." Then followed a note about rubbing the culprit's hand " with sweet butter or dripping" should you have struck too hard.

Dispiriting item, that on resuming his seat the chastised one is a hero to his fellows for the rest of the day. Item, that Master John James Rattray knows she hurts her own hand more than his. Item, that John James promised to be good throughout the session if she would let him thrash the bad ones. Item, that Master T. Sandys, himself under correction, explained to her (the artistic instinct again) how to give the cane a waggle when descending, which would double its nip. Item, that Elsie Dundas offered to receive Francie Crabb's punishment for two snaps. Item, that Master Gavin Dishart, for what he considered the honour of his school, though aware he was imperilling his soul, fought Hendry Dickie of Cathro's for saying Miss Ailie could not draw blood with one stroke.

The effect on Miss Ailie of these mortifying discoveries could be read in the paragraph headed A MOTHER'S METHOD, which was copied from a newspaper. Mrs. E——, it seems, was the mother of four boys (residing at D——), and she subjected them frequently to corporal chastisement without permanent spiritual result. Mrs. E.——, by the advice of another lady, Mrs. K—— (mother of six), then had recourse to the following interesting experiment. Instead of punishing her children physically when they misbehaved, she now in their presence wounded herself by striking her left hand severely with a ruler held in the right. Soon their better natures were touched, and the four implored her to desist, promising with tears never to offend again. From that hour Mrs. E—— had little trouble with her boys.

It was recorded in the blue and white book how Miss Ailie gave this plan a fair trial, but her boys must have been darker characters than Mrs. E——'s, for it merely set them to watching each other, so that they might cry out, " Pandy yourself quick, Miss Ailie; Gavin Dishart's drawing the devil on his slate." Nevertheless, when Miss Ailie announced a return to more conventional methods, Francie was put up (with threats) to say that he suffered agonies of remorse every time she pandied herself for him, but the thing had been organized in a hurry and Francie was insufficiently primed, and on cross-examination he let out that he thought remorse was a swelling of the hands.

Miss Ailie was very humble-minded, and her entries under THE TEACHER TAUGHT were all admonitions for herself. Thus she chided herself for cowardice because " Delicate private reasons have made me avoid all mention of India in the geography classes. Kitty says quite calmly that this is fair neither to our pupils nor to I—— M——. The courage of Kitty in this matter is a constant rebuke to me." Except on a few occasions Mr. McLean found that he was always referred to as I—— M——.

Quite early in the volume Miss Ailie knew that her sister's hold on life was loosening. " How bright the world suddenly seems," Mr. McLean read, "when there is the tiniest improvement in the health of an invalid one loves." Is it laughable that such a note as this is appended to a recipe for beef-tea? " It is surely not very wicked to pretend to Kitty that I keep some of it for myself; she would not take it all if she knew I dined on the beef it was made from." Other entries showed too plainly that Miss Ailie stinted herself of food to provide delicacies for Miss Kitty. No doubt her expenses were alarming her when she wrote this: "An interesting article in the *Mentor* says that nearly all of us eat and drink too much. Were we to mortify our stomachs we should be healthier animals and more capable of sustained thought. The word animal in this connection is coarse, but the article is most impressive, and a crushing reply to Dr. McQueen's assertion that the editor drinks. In the school-room I have frequently found my thoughts of late wandering from classwork, and I hastily ascribed it to sitting up during the night with Kitty or to my habit of listening lest she should be calling for me. Probably I had over-eaten, and I must mortify the stomach. A glass of hot water with half a spoonful of sugar in it is highly recommended as a light supper."

"How long ago it may seem since yesterday!" Do you need to be told on what dark day Miss Ailie discovered that? "I used to pray that I should be taken first, but I was both impious and selfish, for how could fragile Kitty have fought on alone ? "

In time happiness again returned to Miss Ailie ; of all our friends it is the one most reluctant to leave us on this side of the grave. It came at first disguised, in the form of duties, old and new; and stealthily, when Miss Ailie was not looking, it mixed with the small worries and joys that had been events while Miss Kitty lived, and these it converted once more into events, where Miss Ailie found it lurking, and at first she would not take it back to her heart, but it crept in without her knowing. And still there were I—— M——'s letters. "They are all I have to look forward to," she wrote in self-defence. "I shall never write to I—— M—— again," was another entry, but Mr. McLean found on the same page, "I have written to I—— M——, but do not intend posting it," and beneath that was, "God forgive me, I have posted it."

The troubles with arithmetic were becoming more terrible. "I am never *really* sure about the decimals," she wrote.

A Professor of Memory had appeared at the Muckley, and Miss Ailie admits having given him half-a-crown to explain his system to her. But when he was gone she could not remember whether you multiplied everything by ten before dividing by five and subtracting a hundred, or began by dividing and doing something underhand with the cube root. Then Mr. Dishart, who had a microscope, wanted his boy to be taught science, and several experiments were described at length in the book, one of them dealing with a penny, H, and a piston, $X\ Y$, and you do things to the piston "and then the penny comes to the surface." "But it never does," Miss Ailie wrote sorrowfully; perhaps she was glad when Master Dishart was sent to another school.

"Though I teach the girls the pianoforte I find that I cannot stretch my fingers as I used to do. Kitty used to take the music, and I often remember this suddenly when superintending a lesson. It is a pain to me that so many wish to acquire 'The Land o' the Leal,' which Kitty sang so often to I—— M—— at Magenta Cottage."

Even the French, of which Miss Ailie had once been very proud, was slipping from her. "Kitty and I kept up our French by translating I—— M——'s letters and comparing our versions, but now that this stimulus is taken away I find that I am forgetting my French. Or is it only that I am growing old? too old to keep school?" This dread was beginning to haunt Miss Ailie, and the pages between which the blotting-paper lay revealed that she had written to the editor of the *Mentor* asking up to what age he thought a needy gentlewoman had a right to teach. The answer was not given, but her comment on it told everything. "I asked him to be severely truthful, so that I cannot resent his reply. But if I take his advice, how am I to live? And if I do not take it, I fear I am but a stumbling-block in the way of true education."

That is a summary of what Mr. McLean read in the blue and white book; remember, you were warned not to expect much. And Tommy and Gavinia listened, and Tommy said, "I hear no laughing," and Gavinia answered, "But he has quieted down," and upstairs Miss Ailie was on her knees. A time came when Mr. McLean could find something to laugh at in that little pass-book, but it was not then, not even when he reached the end. He left something on the last page instead. At least I think it must have been he : Miss Ailie's tears could not have been so long a-drying.

You may rise, now, Miss Ailie; your prayer is granted.

CHAPTER XXVI

TOMMY REPENTS, AND IS NONE THE WORSE FOR IT

Mr. McLean wrote a few reassuring words to Miss Ailie, and having told Gavinia to give the note to her walked quietly out of the house; he was coming back after he had visited Miss Kitty's grave. Gavinia, however, did not know this, and having delivered the note she returned dolefully to the kitchen to say to Tommy, " His letter maun have been as thraun as himsel', for as soon as she read it, down she plumped on her knees again."

But Tommy was not in the kitchen; he was on the garden-wall watching Miss Ailie's persecutor.

" Would it no be easier to watch him frae the gate?" suggested Gavinia, who had not the true detective instinct.

Tommy disregarded her womanlike question; a great change had come over him since she went upstairs; his head now wobbled on his shoulders like a little balloon that wanted to cut its connection with earth and soar.

" What makes you look so queer?" cried the startled maid. " I thought you was converted."

335

"So I am," he shouted, "I'm more converted than ever, and yet I can do it just the same! Gavinia, I've found a wy!"

He was hurrying off on Mr. McLean's trail, but turned to say, "Gavinia, do you ken wha that man is?"

"Ower weel I ken," she answered, "it's Mr. McLean."

"McLean!" he echoed scornfully, "ay, I've heard that's one of the names he goes by, but hearken, and I'll tell you wha he really is. That's the scoundrel Stroke!"

No wonder Gavinia was flabbergasted. "Wha are you then?" she cried.

"I'm the Champion of Dames," he replied loftily, and before she had recovered from this he was stalking Mr. McLean in the cemetery.

Miss Kitty sleeps in a beautiful hollow called the Basin, but the stone put up to her memory hardly marks the spot now, for with a score of others it was blown on its face by the wind that uprooted so many trees in the Den, and as it fell it lies. From the Basin to the rough road that clings like a belt to the round cemetery dyke is little more than a jump, and shortly after Miss Kitty's grave had been pointed out to him, Mr. McLean was seen standing there hat in hand by a man on the road. This man was Dr. McQueen hobbling home from the Forest Muir; he did not hobble as a rule, but hobble everyone must on that misshapen brae, except Murdoch Gelatley, who, being short in one leg elsewhere, is here the only straight man. McQueen's sharp eyes, however, picked out not only the stranger but Tommy crouching behind Haggert's stone, and him did the doctor's famous crook staff catch in the neck and whisk across the dyke.

"What man is that you're watching, you mysterious loon?" McQueen demanded, curiously; but of course Tommy would not divulge so big a secret. Now the one weakness of this large-hearted old bachelor (perhaps it is a professional virtue) was a devouring inquisitiveness, and he would be troubled until he discovered who was the stranger standing in such obvious emotion by the side of an old grave. "Well, you must come back with me to the surgery, for I want you to run an errand for me," he said testily, hoping to pump the boy by the way, but Tommy dived beneath his stick and escaped. This rasped the doctor's temper, which was unfortunate for Grizel, whom he caught presently peeping in at his surgery window. A dozen times of late she had wondered whether she should ask him to visit her mamma, and though the Painted Lady had screamed in terror at the proposal, being afraid of doctors, Grizel would have ventured ere now, had it not been for her mistaken conviction that he was a hard man, who

would only flout her. It had once come to her
ears that he had said a woman like her mamma
could demoralize a whole town, with other harsh
remarks, doubtless exaggerated in the repetition,
and so he was the last man she dared think of
going to for help, when he should have been the
first. Nevertheless she had come now, and a soft
word from him, such as he gave most readily to
all who were in distress, would have drawn her
pitiful tale from her, but he was in a grumpy
mood, and had heard none of the rumours about
her mother's being ill, which indeed were only
common among the Monypenny children, and his
first words checked her confidences. "What are
you hanging about my open window for?" he
cried sharply.

"Did you think I wanted to steal anything?"
replied the indignant child.

"I won't say but what I had some such thait."

She turned to leave him, but he hooked her with
his staff. "As you're here," he said, "will you go
an errand for me?"

"No," she told him promptly; "I don't like
you."

"There's no love lost between us," he replied,
"for I think you are the dourest lassie I ever
clapped eyes on, but there's no other litlin handy,
so you must do as you are bid, and take this bottle
to Ballingall's."

338

"Is it a medicine bottle?" she asked, with sudden interest.

"Yes, it's medicine. Do you know Ballingall's house in the West town end?"

"Ballingall who has the little school?"

"The same, but I doubt he'll keep school no longer."

"Is he dying?"

"I'm afraid there's no doubt of it. Will you go?"

"I should love to go," she cried.

"Love!" he echoed, looking at her with displeasure. "You can't love to go, so talk no more nonsense, but go, and I'll give you a bawbee."

"I don't want a bawbee," she said. "Do you think they will let me go in to see Ballingall?"

The doctor frowned. "What makes you want to see a dying man?" he demanded.

"I should just love to see him!" she exclaimed, and she added determinedly, "I won't give up the bottle until they let me in."

He thought her an unpleasant, morbid girl, but "that is no affair of mine," he said, shrugging his shoulders, and he gave her the bottle to deliver. Before taking it to Ballingall's, however, she committed a little crime. She bought an empty bottle at the 'Sosh, and poured into it some of the contents of the medicine bottle, which she then filled up with water. She dared try no other way of getting medicine for her mother, and was too

339

ignorant to know that there are different drugs for different ailments.

Grizel not only contrived to get in to see Ballingall, but stayed by his side for several hours, and when she came out it was night-time. On her way home she saw a light moving in the Den, where she had expected to play no more, and she could not prevent her legs from running joyously toward it. So when Corp, rising out of the darkness, deftly cut her throat, she was not so angry as she should have been.

"I'm so glad we are to play again, after all, Corp," she said; but he replied grandly, "Thou little kennest wha you're speaking to, my gentle jade."

He gave a curious hitch to his breeches, but it only puzzled her. "I wear gallowses no more," he explained, lifting his waistcoat to show that his braces now encircled him as a belt, but even then she did not understand. "Know, then," said Corp, sternly, "I am Ben the Boatswain."

"And am I not the Lady Griselda any more?" she asked.

"I'm no sure," he confessed; "but if you are, there's a price on your head."

"What is Tommy?"

"I dinna ken yet, but Gavinia says he telled her he's Champion of Damns. I kenna what Elspeth'll say to that."

340

Grizel was starting for the Lair, but he caught her by the skirt.

"Is he not at the Lair?" she inquired.

"We knowest it not," he answered gravely. "We're looking for't," he added with some awe; "we've been looking for't this three year." Then, in a louder voice, "If you can guide us to it, my pretty trifle, you'll be richly rewarded."

"But where is he? Don't you know?"

"Fine I knowest, but it wouldna be mous to tell you, for I kenna whether you be friend or foe. What's that you 're carrying?"

"It is a — a medicine bottle."

"Gie me a sook!"

"No."

"Just one," begged Corp, "and I'll tell you where he is."

He got his way, and smacked his lips unctuously.

"Now, where is Tommy?"

"Put your face close to mine," said Corp, and then he whispered hoarsely, "He's in a spleet new Lair, writing out bills wi' a' his might, offering five hunder crowns reward for Stroke's head, dead or alive!"

The new haunt was a deserted house, that stood, very damp, near a little waterfall to the east of the Den. Bits of it well planted in the marsh adhere doggedly together to this day, but even then the roof was off and the chimney lay in a heap on the ground, like blankets that have slipped off a bed.

This was the good ship Ailie, lying at anchor, man-of-war, thirty guns, a cart-wheel to steer it by, T. Sandys, commander.

On the following Saturday, Ben the Boatswain piped all hands, and Mr. Sandys delivered a speech of the bluff, straightforward kind that sailors love. Here, unfortunately, it must be condensed. He reminded them that three years had passed since their gracious queen (cheers) sent them into these seas to hunt down the Pretender (hisses). Their ship had been christened the Ailie, because its object was to avenge the insults offered by the Pretender to a lady of that name for whom everyone of them would willingly die. Like all his race the Pretender, or Stroke, as he called himself, was a torment to single women; he had not only stolen all this lady's wealth, but now he wanted to make her walk the plank, a way of getting rid of enemies the mere mention of which set the blood of all honest men boiling (cheers). As yet they had not succeeded in finding Stroke's Lair, though they knew it to be in one of the adjoining islands, but they had suffered many privations, twice their gallant vessel had been burned to the water's edge, once she had been sunk, once blown into the air, but had that dismayed them?

342

Here the Boatswain sent round a whisper, and they all cried loyally, " Ay, ay, sir."

He had now news for them that would warm their hearts like grog. He had not discovered the Lair, but he had seen Stroke, he had spoken to him! Disguised as a boy he had tracked the Jacobite and found him skulking in the house of the unhappy Ailie. After blustering for a little Stroke had gone on his knees and offered not only to cease persecuting this lady but to return to France. Mr. Sandys had kicked him into a standing posture and then left him. But this clemency had been ill repaid. Stroke had not returned to France. He was staying at the Quharity Arms, a Thrums inn, where he called himself McLean. It had gone through the town like wildfire that he had written to someone in Redlintie to send him on another suit of clothes and four dickies. No one suspected his real character, but all noted that he went to the unhappy Ailie's house daily, and there was a town about it. Ailie was but a woman, and women could not defend themselves (" Boatswain, put Grizel in irons if she opens her mouth "), and so the poor thing had been forced to speak to him, and even to go walks with him. Her life was in danger, and before now Mr. Sandys would have taken him prisoner, but the queen had said these words, " Noble Sandys, destroy the Lair," and the best way to discover this horrid spot was to follow

Stroke night and day until he went to it. Then they would burn it to the ground, put him on board the Ailie, up with the jib-boom sail, and away to the Tower of London.

At the words " Tower of London," Ben cried, " Tumble up there ! " which was the signal for three such ringing cheers as only British tars are capable of. Three ? To be exact only two and a half, for the third stopped in the middle, as if the lid had suddenly been put on.

What so startled them was the unexpected appearance in their midst of the very man Tommy had been talking of. Taking a stroll through the Den, Mr. McLean had been drawn toward the ruin by the first cheers, and had arrived in time to learn who and what he really was.

" Stroke ! " gasped one small voice.

The presumptuous man folded his arms. " So, Sandys," he said, in hollow tones, " we meet again ! "

Even Grizel got behind Tommy, and perhaps it was this that gave him spunk to say tremulously, " Wh-what are you doing here ? "

" I have come," replied the ruddy Pretender, " to defy you, ay, proud Sandys, to challenge thee to the deed thou pratest of. I go from here to my Lair. Follow me, if thou darest ! "

He brought his hand down with a bang upon the barrel, laughed disdainfully, and springing over the vessel's side was at once lost in the darkness. Instead of following, all stood transfixed, gazing at the barrel, on which lay five shillings.

"He put them there when he slammed it!"

"Losh behears! there's a shilling to ilka ane o' us."

"I winna touch the siller," said Sandys, moodily.

"What?" cried Gavinia.

"I tell you it's a bribe."

"Do you hear him?" screamed Gavinia. "He says we're no to lay hands on't! Corp, where's your tongue?"

But even in that trying moment Corp's trust in Tommy shone out beautiful and strong. "Dinna be feared, Gavinia," he whispered, "he'll find a w'y."

"Lights out and follow Stroke!" was the order, and the crew at once scattered in pursuit, Mr. Sandys remaining behind a moment to — to put something in his pocket.

Mr. McLean gave them a long chase, walking demurely when lovers were in sight, but at other times doubling, jumping, even standing on eminences and crowing insultingly, like a cock, and not until he had only breath left to chuckle did the stout man vanish from the Den. Elspeth, now a cabin-boy, was so shaken by the realism of the night's adventures that Gavinia (able seaman) took her home, and when Mr. Sandys and his Boatswain met at the Cuttle Well neither could tell where Grizel was.

"She had no business to munt without my leave," Tommy said sulkily.

"No, she hadna. Is she the Lady Griselda yet?"

"Not her, she's the Commander's wife."

Ben shook his head, for this, he felt, was the one thing Tommy could not do. "Well, then," growled Tommy, "if she winna be that, she'll have to serve before the mast, for I tell you plain I'll have no single women on board."

"And what am I, forby Ben the Boatswain?"

"Nothing. Honest men has just one name."

"What! I'm just one single man?" Corp was a little crestfallen. "It's a come down," he said, with a sigh, "mind, I dinna grumble, but it's a come down."

"And you dinna have 'Methinks' now either," Tommy announced pitilessly.

Corp had dreaded this. "I'll be gey an' lonely without it," he said, with some dignity, "and it was the usefulest swear I kent o'. 'Methinks!' I used to roar at Mason Malcolm's collie, and the crittur came in ahint in a swite o' fear. Losh, Tommy, is that you blooding?"

There was indeed an ugly gash on Tommy's hand. "You've been hacking at yoursel' again," said the distressed Corp, who knew that in his enthusiasm Tommy had more than once drawn blood from himself. "When you take it a' so real as that," he said uncomfortably, " I near think we should give it up."

Tommy stamped his foot. " Take tent o' yoursel'!" he cried threateningly. " When I was tracking Stroke I fell in with one of his men, and we had a tussle. He pinked me in the hand, but 't is only a scratch, bah ! He was carrying treasure, and I took it from him."

Ben whistled. " Five shillings ? " he asked, slapping his knee.

" How did you know ? " demanded Tommy, frowning, and then they tried to stare each other down.

" I thought I saw you pouching it," Corp ventured to say.

" Boatswain ! "

" I mean," explained Corp hurriedly, " I mean that I kent you would find a wy. Didest thou kill the Jacobite rebel ? "

" He lies but a few paces off," replied Tommy, " and already the vultures are picking his bones."

" So perish all Victoria's enemies," said Ben the Boatswain, loyally, but a sudden fear made him add, with a complete change of voice, " You dinna chance to ken his name ? "

" Ay, I had marked him before," answered Tommy, " he was called Corp of Corp."

Ben the Boatswain rose, sat down, rose again. " Tommy," he said, wiping his brow with his sleeve, " come awa' hame ! "

347

CHAPTER XXVII

THE LONGER CATECHISM

In the meantime Mr. McLean was walking slowly to the Quharity Arms, fanning his face with his hat, and in the West town end he came upon some boys who had gathered with offensive cries round a girl in a lustre jacket. A wave of his stick put them to flight, but the girl only thanked him with a look, and entered a little house the window of which showed a brighter light than its neighbours. Dr. McQueen came out of this house a moment afterwards, and as the two men now knew each other slightly they walked home together, McLean relating humorously how he had spent the evening. "And though Commander Sandys means to incarcerate me in the Tower of London," he said, "he did me a good service the other day, and I feel an interest in him."

"What did the inventive sacket do?" the doctor asked inquisitively; but McLean, who had referred to the incident of the pass-book, affected not to hear. "Miss Ailie has told me his history," he said, "and that he goes to the University next year."

" Or to the herding," put in McQueen, dryly.

" Yes, I heard that was the alternative, but he should easily carry a bursary; he is a remarkable boy."

" Ay, but I'm no sure that it's the remarkable boys who carry the bursaries. However, if you have taken a fancy to him, you should hear what Mr. Cathro has to say on the subject; for my own part I have been more taken up with one of his band lately than with himself — a lassie, too."

" She who went into that house just before you came out ? "

" The same, and she is the most puzzling bit of womankind I ever fell in with."

" She looked an ordinary girl enough," said Mr. McLean.

The doctor chuckled. " Man," he said, " in my time I have met all kinds of women except ordinary ones. What would you think if I told you that this ordinary girl had been spending three or four hours daily in that house entirely because there was a man dying in it ? "

" Some one she had an affection for ? "

" My certie, no ! I'm afraid it is long since anybody had an affection for shilpit, hirpling, old Ballingall, and as for this lassie Grizel, she had never spoken to him until I sent her on an errand to his house a week ago. He was a single man (like you and me), without womenfolk, a schoolmaster of his own making, and in the smallest way, and his one attraction to her was that he was on his death-bed. Most lassies of her age skirl to get away from the presence of death, but she prigged, sir, fairly prigged, to get into it!"

"Ah, I prefer less uncommon girls," McLean said. "They should not have let her have her wish; it can only do her harm."

"That is another curious thing," replied the doctor. "It does not seem to have done her any harm; rather it has turned her from being a dour, silent crittut into a talkative one, and that, I take it, is a sign of grace."

He sighed, and added: "Not that I can get her to talk of herself and her mother. (There is a mystery about them, you understand.) No, the obstinate brat will tell me nothing on that subject; instead of answering my questions she asks questions of me—an endless rush of questions, and all about Ballingall. How did I know he was dying? When you put your fingers on their wrist, what is it you count? which is the place where the lungs are? when you tap their chest, what do you listen for? are they not dying as long as they can rise now and then, and dress and go out? when they are really dying, do they always know it themselves? If they don't know it, is that a sign that they are not so ill as you think them? When they don't know they are dying, is it best to keep it from them in case they should scream with terror? and so on in a spate of questions, till I called her the Longer Catechism."

"And only morbid curiosity prompted her?"

"Nothing else," said the confident doctor; "if there had been anything else, I should have found it out, you may be sure. However, unhealthily minded though she be, the women who took their turn at Ballingall's bedside were glad of her help."

"The more shame to them," McLean remarked warmly; but the doctor would let no one, save himself, miscall the women of Thrums.

"Ca' canny," he retorted. "The women of this place are as overdriven as the men, from the day they have the strength to turn a pirn-wheel to the day they crawl over their bed-board for the last time, but never yet have I said, ' I need one of you to sit up all night wi' an unweel body,' but what there were half a dozen willing to do it. They are a grand race, sir, and will remain so till they find it out themselves."

"But of what use could a girl of twelve or fourteen be to them?"

"Use!" McQueen cried. "Man, she has been simply a treasure, and but for one thing I would believe it was less a morbid mind than a sort of divine instinct for nursing that took her to Ballingall's bedside. The women do their best in a rough-and-ready way; but, sir, it cowed to see that

351

lassie easying a pillow for Ballingall's head, or changing a sheet without letting in the air, or getting a poultice on his back without disturbing the one on his chest. I had just to let her see how to do these things once, and after that Ballingall complained if any other soul touched him."

" Ah," said McLean, " then perhaps I was uncharitable, and the nurse's instinct is the true explanation."

" No, you're wrong again, though I might have been taken in as well as you but for the one thing I spoke of. Three days ago Ballingall had a ghost of a chance of pulling through, I thought, and I told the lassie that if he did, the credit would be mainly hers. You'll scarcely believe it, but, upon my word, she looked disappointed rather than pleased, and she said to me, quite reproachfully, ' You told me he was sure to die!' What do you make of that ? "

" It sounds unnatural."

" It does, and so does what followed. Do you know what straiking is ? "

" Arraying the corpse for the coffin, laying it out, in short, is it not ? "

" Ay, ay. Well, it appears that Grizel had prigged with the women to let her be present at Ballingall's straiking, and they had refused."

" I should think so," exclaimed McQueen, with a shudder.

"But that's not all. She came to me in her difficulty, and said that if I didna promise her this privilege, she would nurse Ballingall no more."

"Ugh! That shows at least that pity for him had not influenced her."

"No, she cared not a doit for him. I question if she's the kind that could care for anyone. It's plain by her thrawn look when you speak to her about her mother that she has no affection even for her. However, there she was, prepared to leave Ballingall to his fate if I did not grant her request, and I had to yield to her."

"You promised?"

"I did, sore against the grain, but I accept the responsibility. You are pained, but you don't know what a good nurse means to a doctor."

"Well?"

"Well, he died after all, and the straiking is going on now. You saw her go in."

"I think you could have been excused for breaking your word and turning her out."

"To tell the truth," said the doctor, "I had the same idea when I saw her enter, and I tried to shoo her to the door, but she cried, 'You promised, you *can't* break a promise!' and the morbid brat that she is looked so horrified at the very notion of anybody's breaking a promise that I slunk away as if she had right on her side."

"No wonder the little monster is unpopular,"

was McLean's comment. "The children here-
about seem to take to her as little as I do, for I
had to drive away some who were molesting her.
I am sorry I interfered now."

"I can tell you why they t'nead her," replied
the doctor, and he repeated the little that was
known in Thrums of the Painted Lady. "And,
you see, the womenfolk are mad because they can
find out so little about her, where she got her
money, for instance, and who are the 'gentlemen'
that are said to visit her at Double Dykes. They
have tried many ways of drawing Grizel, from
heckle biscuits and parlies to a slap in the face,
but neither by coaxing nor squeezing will you get
an egg out of a sweer hen, and so they found.
'The dour little limmer,' they say, 'stalking about
wi' all her blinds down,' and they are slow to interfere when their laddies call her names. It's a
pity for herself that she's not more communicative,
for if she would just satisfy the women's curiosity
she would find them full of kindness. A terrible
thing, Mr. McLean is curiosity. The Bible says
that the love of money is the root of all evil, but
we must ask Mr. Dishart if love of money is not a
misprint for curiosity. And you won't find men
boring their way into other folk's concerns; it is a
woman's failing, essentially a woman's." This was
the doctor's pet topic, and he pursued it until they
had to part. He had opened his door and was

about to enter when he saw Gavinia passing on her way home from the Den.

"Come here, my lass," he called to her, and then said inquisitively, " I'm told Mr. McLean is at his tea with Miss Ailie every day ? "

"And it's true," replied Gavinia, in huge delight, "and what's more, she has given him some presents."

" You say so, lassie !   What were they now ? "

" I dinna ken," Gavinia had to admit, dejectedly.   "She took them out o' the ottoman, and it has aye been kept locked."

McQueen looked very knowingly at her. "Will he, think you ? " he asked mysteriously.

The maid seemed to understand, for she replied promptly, " I hope he will."

"But he hasna speired her as yet, you think ? "

"No," she said, "no, but he calls her Ailie, and wi' the gentry it's but one loup frae that to speiring."

" Maybe," answered the doctor, " but it's a loup they often bogle at. I'se uphaud he's close on fifty, Gavinia ? "

" There's no denying he is by his best," she said regretfully, and then added, with spirit, " but Miss Ailie's no heavy, and in thae grite arms o' his he could daidle her as if she were an infant."

This bewildered McQueen, and he asked," What are you blethering about, Gavinia ? " to which she

replied, regally, " Wha carries me, wears me ? "
The doctor concluded that it must be Den language.

"And I hope he's good enough for her," continued Miss Ailie's warm-hearted maid, " for she
deserves a good ane."

"She does," McQueen agreed heartily, "ay,
and I believe he is, for he breathes through his
nose instead of through his mouth; and let me
tell you, Gavinia, that's the one thing to be sure
of in a man before you take him for better or
worse."

The astounded maid replied, " I'll ken better
things than that about my lad afore I take him,"
but the doctor assured her that it was the box
which held them all, "though you maun tell no
one, lassie, for it's my one discovery in five and
thirty years of practice."

Seeing that, despite his bantering tone, he was
speaking seriously, she pressed him for his meaning, but he only replied sadly, "You're like the
rest, Gavinia; I see it breaking out on you in
spots."

" An illness ! " she cried, in alarm.

" Ay, lassie, an illness called curiosity. I had
just been telling Mr. McLean that curiosity is essentially a woman's ailment, and up you come
ahint to prove it." He shook a finger at her re-
provingly, and was probably still reflecting on

woman's ways when Grizel walked home at midnight breathing through her nose, and Tommy fell asleep with his mouth open. For Tommy could never have stood the doctor's test of a man. In the painting of him, aged twenty-four, which was exhibited in the Royal Academy, his lips meet firmly, but no one knew save himself how he gasped after each sitting.

CHAPTER XXVIII

THE ottoman whence, as Gavinia said, Miss Ailie produced the presents she gave to Mr. McLean stood near the door of the blue-and-white room, with a reel of thread between, to keep them apart forever. Except on washing days it was of a genteel appearance, for though but a wooden kist, it had a gay outer garment with frills, which Gavinia starched, and beneath this was apparel of a private character that tied with tapes. When Miss Ailie, pins in her mouth, was on her knees arraying the ottoman, it might almost have been mistaken for a female child.

The contents of the ottoman were a few trivial articles sewn or knitted by Miss Kitty during her last illness, "just to keep me out of languor," she would explain wistfully to her sister. She never told Miss Ailie that they were intended for any special person; on the contrary she said, "Perhaps you may find someone they will be useful to," but almost without her knowing it they always grew into something that would be useful to Ivie McLean.

358

"The remarkable thing is that they are an exact fit," the man said about the slippers, and Miss Ailie nodded, but she did not think it remarkable.

There were also two fluffy little bags, and Miss Ailie had to explain their use. "If you put your feet into them in bed," she faltered, "they — they keep you warm."

McLean turned hastily to something else, a smoking-cap. "I scarcely think this can have been meant for me," he said; "you have forgotten how she used to chide me for smoking."

Miss Ailie had not forgotten. "But in a way," she replied, flushing a little, "we — that is, Kitty — could not help admiring you for smoking. There is something so — so dashing about it."

"I was little worth all the friendship you two gave me, Ailie," he told her humbly, and he was nearly saying something to her then that he had made up his mind to say. The time came a few days later. They had been walking together on the hill, and on their return to the Dove-cot he had insisted, "in his old imperious way," on coming in to tea. Hearing talking in the kitchen, Miss Ailie went along the passage to discover what company her maid kept; but before she reached the door, which was ajar, she turned as if she had heard something dreadful and hurried upstairs, signing to Mr. McLean, with imploring eyes, to follow her. This at once sent him to the kitchen door.

359

Gavinia was alone. She was standing in the middle of the floor, with one arm crooked as if making believe that another's arm rested on it, and over her head was a little muslin window-blind, representing a bride's veil. Thus she was two persons, but she was also a third, who addressed them in clerical tones.

"Ivie McLean," she said, as solemnly as though she were the Rev. Mr. Dishart, "do you take this woman to be thy lawful wedded wife?" With almost indecent haste she answered herself, "I do."

"Alison Cray," she said next, "do you take this man to be thy lawful wedded husband?" "I do."

Just then the door shut softly; and Gavinia ran to see who had been listening, with the result that she hid herself in the coal-cellar.

While she was there, Miss Ailie and Mr. McLean were sitting in the blue-and-white room very self-conscious, and Miss Ailie was speaking confusedly of anything and everything, saying more in five minutes than had served for the previous hour, and always as she slackened she read an intention in his face that started her tongue upon another journey. But, "Timid Ailie," he said at last, "do you think you can talk me down?" and then she gave him a look of reproach that turned treacherously into one of appeal, but he had the hardihood to continue: "Ailie, do you need to be told what I want to say?"

Miss Ailie stood quite still now, a stiff, thick figure, with a soft, plain face and nervous hands. "Before you speak," she said nervously, "I have something to tell you that — perhaps then you will not say it.

"I have always led you to believe," she began, trembling, "that I am forty-nine. I am fifty-one."

He would have spoken, but the look of appeal came back to her face, asking him to make it easier for her by saying nothing. She took a pair of spectacles from her pocket, and he divined what this meant before she spoke. "I have avoided letting you see that I need them," she said. "You — men don't like — " She tried to say it all in a rush, but the words would not come.

"I am beginning to be a little deaf," she went on. "To deceive you about that, I have sometimes answered you without really knowing what you said."

"Anything more, Ailie?"

"My accomplishments — they were never great, but Kitty and I thought my playing of classical pieces — my fingers are not sufficiently pliable now. And I — I forget so many things."

"But, Ailie —— "

"Please let me tell you. I was reading a book, a story, last winter, and one of the characters, an old maid, was held up to ridicule in it for many little peculiarities that — that I recognized as my own. They had grown upon me without my knowing that they had made me ridiculous, and now I — I have tried, but I cannot alter them."

" Is that all, Ailie ? "

" No."

The last seemed the hardest to say. Dusk had come on, and they could not see each other well. She asked him to light the lamp, and his back was toward her while he did it, wondering a little at her request. When he turned, her hands rose like cowards to hide her head, but she pulled them down. " Do you not see ? " she said.

" I see that you have done something to your hair," he answered; " I liked it best the other way."

Most people would have liked it best the other way. There was still a good deal of it, but the " bun " in which it ended had gone strangely small. " The rest was false," said Miss Ailie, with a painful effort; " at least, it is my own, but it came out when — when Kitty died."

She stopped, but he was silent. " That is all now," she said softly, and she waited for him to speak if he chose. He turned his head away sharply, and Miss Ailie mistook his meaning. If she gave one little sob — Well, it was but one, and then all the glory of womanhood came rushing to her aid, and it unfurled its flag over her, whispering, " Now, sweet daughter, now, strike for me," and she raised her head gallantly, and for a moment in her life the old school-mistress was a queen. " I shall ring for tea," she said, quietly, and without a tremor; "do you think there is anything so refreshing after a walk as a dish of tea?"

She rang the bell, but its tinkle only made Gavinia recede farther into the cellar, and that summons has not been answered to this day, and no one seems to care, for while the wires were still vibrating Mr. McLean had asked Miss Ailie to forgive him and marry him.

Miss Ailie said she would, but, "Oh," she cried, "ten years ago it might have been my Kitty. I would that it had been Kitty!"

Miss Ailie was dear to him now, and ten years is a long time, and men are vain. Mr. McLean replied, quite honestly, "I am not sure that I did not always like you best," but that hurt her, and he had to unsay the words.

"I was a thoughtless fool ten years ago," he said bitterly, and Miss Ailie's answer came strangely from such timid lips. "Yes, you were!" she exclaimed passionately, and all the wrath, long pent up, with very different feelings, in her gentle bosom, against the man who should have adored her Kitty, leapt at that reproachful cry to her mouth and eyes, and so passed out of her forever.

CHAPTER XXIX

So Miss Ailie could be brave, but what a poltroon she was also! Three calls did she make on dear friends, ostensibly to ask how a cold was or to instruct them in the new device in Shetland wool, but really to announce that she did not propose keeping school after the end of the term — because — in short, Mr. Ivie McLean and she — that is, he — and so on. But though she had planned it all out so carefully, with at least three capital ways of leading up to it, and knew precisely what they would say, and pined to hear them say it, on each occasion shyness conquered and she came away with the words unspoken. How she despised herself, and how Mr. McLean laughed! He wanted to take the job off her hands by telling the news to Dr. McQueen, who could be depended on to spread it through the town, and Miss Ailie discovered with horror that his simple plan was to say, "How are you, Doctor? I just looked in to tell you that Miss Ailie and I are to be married. Good afternoon." The audacity of

364

this captivated Miss Ailie even while it outraged her sense of decency. To Redlintie went Mr. McLean, and returning next day, drew from his pocket something which he put on Miss Ailie's finger, and then she had the idea of taking off her left glove in church, which would have announced her engagement as loudly as though Mr. Dishart had included it in his pulpit intimations. Religion, however, stopped her when she had got the little finger out, and the Misses Finlayson, who sat behind and knew she had an itchy something inside her glove, concluded that it was her threepenny for the plate. As for Gavinia, like others of her class in those days, she had never heard of engagement rings, and so it really seemed as if Mr. McLean must call on the doctor after all. But "No," said he, "I hit upon a better notion to-day in the Den," and to explain this notion he produced from his pocket a large, vulgar bottle, which shocked Miss Ailie, and indeed that bottle had not passed through the streets uncommented on.

Mr. McLean having observed this bottle afloat on the Silent Pool, had fished it out with his stick, and its contents set him chuckling. They consisted of a sheet of paper which stated that the bottle was being flung into the sea in lat. 20, long. 40, by T. Sandys, Commander of the Ailie, then among the breakers. Sandys had little hope of weathering the gale, but he was indifferent to his own fate so long as his enemy did not escape, and he called upon whatsoever loyal subjects of the queen should find this document to sail at once to lat. 20, long. 40, and there cruise till they had captured the Pretender, *alias* Stroke, and destroyed his Lair. A somewhat unfavourable personal description of Stroke was appended, with a map of the coast, and a stern warning to all loyal subjects not to delay, as one Ailie was in the villain's hands, and he might kill her any day. Victoria Regina would give five hundred crowns for his head. The letter ended in manly style with the writer's sending an affecting farewell message to his wife and little children.

"And so while we are playing ourselves," said Mr. McLean to Miss Ailie, "your favourite is seeking my blood."

"Our favourite," interposed the school-mistress; and he accepted the correction, for neither of them could forget that their present relations might have been very different had it not been for Tommy's faith in the pass-book. The boy had shown a knowledge of the human heart, in Miss Ailie's opinion, that was simply wonderful; inspiration she called it, and though Ivie thought it a happy accident, he did not call it so to her. Tommy's father had been the instrument in bringing these two together originally, and now Tommy had brought them together again; there was fate in it, and if the boy was of the right stuff McLean meant to reward him.

"I see now," he said to Miss Ailie, "a way of getting rid of our fearsome secret and making my peace with Sandys at one fell blow." He declined to tell her more, but presently he sought Gavinia, who dreaded him nowadays because of his disconcerting way of looking at her inquiringly and saying "I do!"

"You don't happen to know, Gavinia," he asked, "whether the good ship Ailie weathered the gale of the 15th instant? If it did," he went on, "Commander Sandys will learn something to his advantage from a bottle that is to be cast into the ocean this evening."

Gavinia thought she heard the chink of another five shillings, and her mouth opened so wide that a chaffinch could have built therein. "Is he to look for a bottle in the pond?" she asked eagerly.

"I do," replied McLean with such solemnity that she again retired to the coal-cellar.

That evening Mr. McLean cast a bottle into the Silent Pool, and subsequently called on Mr. Cathro, to whom he introduced himself as one interested in Master Thomas Sandys. He was heartily received, but at the name of Tommy, Cathro heaved a sigh that could not pass unnoticed. "I see you don't find him an angel," said Mr. McLean, politely.

"'Deed, sir, there are times when I wish he was an angel," the dominie replied so viciously that McLean laughed. "And I grudge you that laugh," continued Cathro, "for your Tommy Sandys has taken from me the most precious possession a teacher can have — my sense of humour."

"He strikes me as having a considerable sense of humour himself."

"Well, he may, Mr. McLean, for he has gone off with all mine. But bide a wee till I get in the tumblers, and I'll tell you the latest about him — if what you want to hear is just the plain exasperating truth.

"His humour that you spoke of," resumed the schoolmaster presently, addressing his words to the visitor, and his mind to a toddy-ladle of horn, "is ill to endure in a school where the understanding is that the dominie makes all the jokes (except on examination day, when the ministers get their yearly fling), but I think I like your young friend worst when he is deadly serious. He is constantly playing some new part — playing is hardly the word though, for into each part he puts an earnestness that cheats even himself, until he takes to another. I suppose you want me to give you some idea of his character, and I could tell you what it is at any particular moment; but it changes, sir, I do assure you, almost as quickly as the circusrider flings off his layers of waistcoats. A single puff of wind blows him from one character to another, and he may be noble and vicious, and a tyrant and a slave, and hard as granite and melting as butter in the sun, all in one forenoon. All you can be sure of is that whatever he is, he will be it in excess."

"But I understood," said McLean, "that at present he is solely engaged on a war of extermination in the Den."

"Ah, those exploits, I fancy, are confined to Saturday nights, and unfortunately his Saturday debauch does not keep him sober for the rest of the week, which we demand of respectable characters in these parts. For the last day or two, for instance, he has been in mourning."

"I had not heard of that."

"No, I daresay not, and I'll give you the facts, if you'll fill your glass first. But perhaps —" here the dominie's eyes twinkled as if a gleam of humour had been left him after all — "perhaps you have been more used of late to ginger wine?"

The visitor received the shot impassively, as if he did not know he had been hit, and Cathro proceeded with his narrative. "Well, for a day or two Tommy Sandys has been coming to the school in a black jacket with crape on the cuffs, and not only so, he has sat quiet and forlorn-like at his desk, as if he had lost some near and dear relative. Now I knew that he had not, for his only relative

is a sister whom you may have seen at the Hanky
School, and both she and Aaron Latta are hearty.
Yet, sir (and this shows the effect he has on me),
though I was puzzled and curious, I dared not
ask for an explanation."

"But why not?" was the visitor's natural question.

"Because, sir, he is such a mysterious little
sacket," replied Cathro, testily, "and so clever at
leading you into a hole, that it's not chancey to
meddle with him, and I could see through the
corner of my eye that, for all this woeful face, he
was proud of it, and hoped I was taking note.
For though sometimes his emotion masters him
completely, at other times he can step aside, as it
were, and take an approving look at it. That is
a characteristic of him, and not the least maddening one."

"But you solved the mystery somehow, I suppose?"

"I got at the truth to-day by an accident, or
rather my wife discovered it for me. She happened
to call in at the school on a domestic matter I need
not trouble you with (sal, she needna have troubled
me with it either!), and on her way up the yard she
noticed a laddie called Lewis Doig playing with
other ungodly youths at the game of kickbonnety.
Lewis's father, a gentleman farmer, was buried
jimply a fortnight since, and such want of respect

for his memory made my wife give the loon a
dunt on the head with a pound of sugar, which
she had just bought at the 'Sosh. He turned on
her, ready to scart or spit or run, as seemed wisest,
and in a klink her woman's eye saw what mine had
overlooked, that he was not even wearing a black
jacket. Well, she told him what the slap was for,
and his little countenance cleared at once. ' Oh,'
says he, ' that's all right, Tommy and me has arranged it,' and he pointed blithely to a corner of
the yard where Tommy was hunkering by himself
in Lewis's jacket, and wiping his mournful eyes
with Lewis's hanky. I daresay you can jalouse
the rest, but I kept Lewis behind after the school
skailed, and got a full confession out of him. He
had tried hard, he gave me to understand, to mourn
fittingly for his father, but the kickbonnety season
being on, it was up-hill work, and he was relieved
when Tommy volunteered to take it off his hands.
Tommy's offer was to swop jackets every morning
for a week or two, and thus properly attired to do
the mourning for him."

The dominie paused, and regarded his guest
quizzically. " Sir," he said at length, " laddies are
a queer growth; I assure you, there was no persuading Lewis that it was not a right and honourable compact."

" And what payment," asked McLean, laughing,
"did Tommy demand from Lewis for this service?"

"Not a farthing, sir — which gives another uncanny glint into his character. When he wants money, there's none so crafty at getting it, but he did this for the pleasure of the thing, or, as he said to Lewis, 'to feel what it would be like.' That, I tell you, is the nature of the sacket; he has a devouring desire to try on other folk's feelings, as if they were so many suits of clothes."

"And from your account he makes them fit him too."

"My certie, he does, and a lippie in the bonnet more than that."

So far the schoolmaster had spoken frankly, even with an occasional grin at his own expense, but his words came reluctantly when he had to speak of Tommy's prospects at the bursary examinations. "I would rather say nothing on that head," he said, almost coaxingly, "for the laddie has a year to reform in yet, and it's never safe to prophesy."

"Still I should have thought that you could guess pretty accurately how the boys you mean to send up in a year's time are likely to do? You have had a long experience, and, I am told, a glorious one."

"'Deed, there's no denying it," answered the dominie, with a pride he had won the right to wear. "If all the ministers, for instance, I have turned out in this bit school were to come back together, they could hold the General Assembly in the square."

He lay back in his big chair, a complacent dominie again. "Guess the chances of my laddies!" he cried, forgetting what he had just said, and that there was a Tommy to bother him. "I tell you, sir, that's a matter on which I'm never deceived. I can tell the results so accurately that a wise Senatus would give my lot the bursaries I say they'll carry, without setting them down to examination-papers at all." And for the next half-hour he was reciting cases in proof of his sagacity.

"Wonderful!" chimed in McLean. "I see it is evident you can tell me how Tommy Sandys will do;" but at that Cathro's rush of words again subsided into a dribble.

"He's the worst Latinist that ever had the impudence to think of bursaries," he groaned.

"And his Greek?" asked McLean, helping on the conversation as far as possible.

"His Greek, sir, could be packed in a pill-box."

"That does not sound promising. But the best mathematicians are sometimes the worst linguists."

"His Greek is better than his mathematics," said Cathro, and he fell into lamentation. "I have had no luck lately," he sighed. "The laddies I have to prepare for college are second-raters, and the vexing thing is, that when a real scholar is reared in Thrums, instead of his being handed over to me for the finishing, they send him to Mr. Ogilvy in Glenquharity. Did Miss Ailie ever mention

Gavin Dishart to you — the minister's son? I just craved to get the teaching of that laddie; he was the kind you can cram with learning till there's no room left for another spoonful, and they bude send him to Mr. Ogilvy, and you'll see he'll stand high above my loons in the bursary list. And then Ogilvy will put on sic airs that there will be no enduring him. Ogilvy and I, sir, we are engaged in an everlasting duel; when we send students to the examinations, it is we two who are the real competitors. But what chance have I, when he is represented by a Gavin Dishart and my man is Tommy Sandys?"

McLean was greatly disappointed. "Why send Tommy up at all if he is so backward?" he said. "You are sure you have not exaggerated his deficiencies?"

"Well, not much, at any rate. But he baffles me; one day I think him a perfect numskull, and the next he makes such a show of the small drop of scholarship he has that I'm not sure but what he may be a genius."

"That sounds better. Does he study hard?"

"Study! He is the most careless whelp that ever —— "

"But if I were to give him an inducement to study?"

"Such as?" asked Cathro, who could at times be as inquisitive as the doctor.

374

"We need not go into that. But suppose it appealed to him?"

Cathro considered. "To be candid," he said, "I don't think he could study, in the big meaning of the word. I daresay I'm wrong, but I have a feeling that whatever knowledge that boy acquires he will dig out of himself. There is something inside him, or so I think at times, that is his master, and rebels against book-learning. No, I can't tell what it is; when we know that, we shall know the real Tommy."

"And yet," said McLean, curiously, "you advise his being allowed to compete for a bursary. That, if you will excuse my saying so, sounds foolish to me."

"It can't seem so foolish to you," replied Cathro, scratching his head, "as it seems to me six days in seven."

"And you know that Aaron Latta has sworn to send him to the herding if he does not carry a bursary. Surely the wisest course would be to apprentice him now to some trade ——"

"What trade would not be the worse of him? He would cut off his fingers with a joiner's saw, and smash them with a mason's mell; put him in a brot behind a counter, and in some grand, magnanimous mood he would sell off his master's things for nothing; make a clerk of him, and he would only ravel the figures; send him to the soldiering, and he would have a sudden impulse to fight on the wrong side. No, no, Miss Ailie says he has a gift for the ministry, and we must cling to that."

In thus sheltering himself behind Miss Ailie, where he had never skulked before, the dominie showed how weak he thought his position, and he added, with a brazen laugh, " Then if he does distinguish himself at the examinations I can take the credit for it, and if he comes back in disgrace I shall call you to witness that I only sent him to them at her instigation."

" All which," maintained McLean, as he put on his topcoat, " means that somehow, against your better judgment, you think he may distinguish himself after all."

" You've found me out," answered Cathro, half relieved, half sorry. " I had no intention of telling you so much, but as you have found me out I'll make a clean breast of it. Unless something unexpected happens to the laddie — unless he take to playing at scholarship as if it were a Jacobite rebellion, for instance — he shouldna have the ghost of a chance of a bursary; and if he were any other boy as ill-prepared I should be ashamed to send him up, but he is Tommy Sandys, you see, and — it is a terrible thing to say, but it's Gospel truth, it's Gospel truth — I'm trusting to the possibility of his diddling the examiners ! "

It was a startling confession for a conscientious dominie, and Cathro flung out his hands as if to withdraw the words, but his visitor would have no tampering with them. "So that sums up Tommy, so far as you know him," he said, as he bade his host good-night.

"It does," Cathro admitted grimly, "but if what you wanted was a written certificate of character I should like to add this, that never did any boy sit on my forms whom I had such a pleasure in thrashing."

CHAPTER XXX

END OF THE JACOBITE RISING

In the small hours of the following night the pulse of Thrums stopped for a moment, and then went on again, but the only watcher remained silent, and the people rose in the morning without knowing that they had lost one of their number while they slept. In the same ignorance they toiled through a long day.

It was a close October day in the end of a summer that had lingered to give the countryside nothing better than a second crop of haws. Beneath the beeches leaves lay in yellow heaps like sliced turnip, and over all the strath was a pink haze; the fields were singed brown, except where a recent ploughing gave them a mourning border. From early morn men, women and children (Tommy among them) were in the fields taking up their potatoes, half-a-dozen gatherers at first to every drill, and by noon it seemed a dozen, though the new-comers were but stout sacks, now able to stand alone. By-and-by heavy-laden carts were trailing into Thrums, dog-tired toilers hanging on

378

behind, not to be dragged, but for an incentive to keep them trudging, boys and girls falling asleep on top of the load, and so neglecting to enjoy the ride which was their recompense for lifting. A growing mist mixed with the daylight, and still there were a few people out, falling over their feet with fatigue; it took silent possession, and then the shadowy forms left in the fields were motionless and would remain there until carted to garrets and kitchen corners and other winter quarters on Monday morning. There were few gadabouts that Saturday night. Washings were not brought in, though Mr. Dishart had preached against the unseemly sight of linen hanging on the line on the Sabbath-day. Innes, stravaiging the square and wynds in his apple-cart, jingled his weights in vain, unable to shake even moneyed children off their stools; and when at last he told his beast to go home, they took with them all the stir of the town. Family exercise came on early in many houses, and as the gude wife handed her man the Bible she said entreatingly, "A short ane." After that one might have said that no earthly knock could bring them to their doors, yet within an hour the town was in a ferment.

When Tommy and Elspeth reached the Den the mist lay so thick that they had to feel their way through it to the Ailie, where they found Gavinia alone and scared. "Was you peeping in, trying to fleg me twa three minutes syne?" she asked eagerly, and when they shook their heads, she looked cold with fear. "As sure as death," she said, "there was some living thing standing there; I couldna see it for the rime, but I heard it breathing hard."

Tommy felt Elspeth's hand begin to tremble, and he said "McLean!" hastily, though he knew that McLean had not yet left the Quharity Arms. Next moment Corp arrived with another story as unnerving.

"Has Grizel no come yet?" he asked, in a troubled voice. "Tommy, hearken to this, a light has been burning in Double Dykes and the door swinging open a' day! I saw it mysel', and so did Willum Dods."

"Did you go close?"

"Na faags! Willum was hol'ing and I was lifting, so we hadna time in the daylight, and wha would venture near the Painted Lady's house on sic a night?"

Even Tommy felt uneasy, but when Gavinia cried, "There's something uncanny in being out the night; tell us what was in Mr. McLean's bottle, Tommy, and syne we'll run hame," he became Commander Sandys again, and replied blankly, "What bottle?"

"The ane I warned you he was to fling into the water; dinna dare tell me you hinna got it."

"I know not what thou art speaking about," said Tommy; "but it's a queer thing, it's a queer thing, Gavinia"—here he fixed her with his terrifying eye—"that I happen to have found a— another bottle," and still glaring at her he explained that he had found this bottle floating on the horizon. It contained a letter to him, which he now read aloud. It was signed " The Villain Stroke, his mark," and announced that the writer, "tired of this relentless persecution," had determined to reform rather than be killed. " Meet me at the Cuttle Well, on Saturday, when the eight-o'clock bell is ringing," he wrote, "and I shall there make you an offer for my freedom."

The crew received this communication with shouts, Gavinia's cry of " Five shillings, if no ten!" expressing the general sentiment, but it would not have been like Tommy to think with them. "You poor things," he said, " you just believe everything you're telled! How do I know that this is not a trick of Stroke's to bring me here when he is some other gait working mischief? "

Corp was impressed, but Gavinia said short-sightedly, " There's no sign o't."

" There's ower much sign o't," retorted Tommy. "What's this story about Double Dykes? And how do we ken that there hasna been foul wark there, and this man at the bottom o't? I tell you, before the world's half an hour older I'll find out," and he looked significantly at Corp, who answered, quaking, " I winna gang by mysel', no, Tommy, I winna ! "

So Tommy had to accompany him, saying valiantly, " I'm no feared, and this rime is fine for hodding in," to which Corp replied as firmly, " Neither am I, and we can aye keep touching cauld iron." Before they were half-way down the Double Dykes they got a thrill, for they realised simultaneously that they were being followed. They stopped and gripped each other hard, but now they could hear nothing.

" The Painted Lady ! " Corp whispered.

" Stroke ! " Tommy replied as cautiously. He was excited rather than afraid, and had the pluck to cry, " Wha's that ? I see you ! " but no answer came back through the mist, and now the boys had a double reason for pressing forward.

" Can you see the house, Corp ? "

" It should be here about, but it's smored in rime."

" I'm touching the paling. I ken the road to the window now."

" Hark ! What's that ? "

It sounded like devil's music in front of them, and they fell back until Corp remembered, " It maun be the door swinging open, and squealing and moaning on its hinges. Tommy, I take ill wi' that. What can it mean ? "

382

HOUSE IN THRUMS WHERE MR. BARRIE
WAS BORN.
From a photograph.

" I'm here to find out." They reached the window where Tommy had watched once before, and looking in together saw the room plainly by the light of a lamp which stood on the spinet. There was no one inside, but otherwise Tommy noticed little change. The fire was out, having evidently burned itself done, the bedclothes were in some disorder. To avoid the creaking door, the boys passed round the back of the house to the window of the other room. This room was without a light, but its door stood open, and sufficient light came from the kitchen to show that it also was untenanted. It seemed to have been used as a lumber-room.

The boys turned to go, passing near the front of the empty house, where they shivered and stopped, mastered by a feeling they could not have explained. The helpless door, like the staring eyes of a dead person, seemed to be calling to them to shut it, and Tommy was about to steal forward for this purpose when Corp gripped him and whispered that the light had gone out. It was true, though Tommy disbelieved until they had returned to the east window to make sure.

"There maun be folk in the hoose, Tommy!"

"You saw it was toom. The lamp had gone out itself, or else — what's that?"

It was the unmistakable closing of a door, softly but firmly. "The wind has blown it to," they

tried to persuade themselves, though aware that
there was not sufficient wind for this. After a long
period of stillness they gathered courage to go to the
door and shake it. It was not only shut, but locked.

On their way back through the Double Dykes
they were silent, listening painfully, but hearing
nothing. But when they reached the Coffin Brig,
Tommy said, "Dinna say nothing about this to
Elspeth, it would terrify her;" he was always so
thoughtful for Elspeth.

"But what do you think o't a'?" Corp said, imploringly.

"I winna tell you yet," replied Tommy, cautiously.

When they boarded the Ailie, where the two
girls were very glad to see them again, the eight-
o'clock bell had begun to ring, and thus Tommy
had a reasonable excuse for hurrying his crew to
the Cuttle Well without saying anything of his
expedition to Double Dykes, save that he had not
seen Grizel. At the Well they had not long to
wait before Mr. McLean suddenly appeared out
of the mist, and to their astonishment Miss Ailie
was leaning on his arm. She was blushing and
smiling too, in a way pretty to see, though it
spoilt the effect of Stroke's statement.

The first thing Stroke did was to give up his
sword to Tommy and to apologise for its being an
umbrella on account of the unsettled state of the

weather, and then Corp led three cheers, the captain alone declining to join in, for he had an uneasy feeling that he was being ridiculed.

"But I thought there were five of you," Mr. McLean said; "where is the fifth?"

"You ken best," replied Tommy, sulkily, and sulky he remained throughout the scene, because he knew he was not the chief figure in it. Having this knowledge to depress him, it is to his credit that he bore himself with dignity throughout, keeping his crew so well in hand that they dared not give expression to their natural emotions.

"As you are aware, Mr. Sandys," McLean began solemnly, "I have come here to sue for pardon. It is not yours to give, you reply, the Queen alone can pardon, and I grant it; but, sir, is it not well known to all of us that you can get anything out of her you like?"

Tommy's eyes roved suspiciously, but the suppliant proceeded in the same tone. "What are my offences? The first is that I have been bearing arms (unwittingly) against the Throne; the second, that I have brought trouble to the lady by my side, who has the proud privilege of calling you her friend. But, Sandys, such amends as can come from an erring man I now offer to make most contritely. Intercede with Her Majesty on my behalf, and on my part I promise to war against her no more. I am willing to settle down in the neighbouring town as a law-abiding citizen, whom you can watch with eagle eye. Say, what more wouldst thou of the unhappy Stuart?"

But Tommy would say nothing; he only looked doubtfully at Miss Ailie, and that set McLean off again. "You ask what reparation I shall make to this lady? Sandys, I tell thee that here also thou hast proved too strong for me. In the hope that she would plead for me with you, I have been driven to offer her my hand in marriage, and she is willing to take me if thou grantest thy consent."

At this Gavinia jumped with joy, and then cried, "Up wi' her!" words whose bearing the school-mistress fortunately did not understand. All save Tommy looked at Miss Ailie, and she put her arm on Mr. McLean's, and — yes, it was obvious, Miss Ailie was a lover at the Cuttle Well at last, like so many others. She had often said that the Den parade was vulgar, but she never said it again.

It was unexpected news to Tommy, but that was not what lowered his head in humiliation now. In the general rejoicing he had been nigh forgotten; even Elspeth was hanging in Miss Ailie's skirts, Gavinia had eyes for none but lovers, Corp was rapturously examining five half-crowns that had been dropped into his hands for distribution. Had Tommy given an order now, who would have obeyed it? His power was gone, his crew would not listen to another word against Mr. McLean.

"Tommy thought Mr. McLean hated you!" said Elspeth to Miss Ailie.

"It was queer you made sic a mistake!" said Corp to Tommy.

"Oh, the tattie-doolie!" cried Gavinia.

So they knew that Mr. McLean had only been speaking sarcastically; of a sudden they saw through and despised their captain. Tears of mortification rose in Tommy's eyes, and kind-hearted Miss Ailie saw them, and she thought it was her lover's irony that made him smart. She had said little hitherto, but now she put her hand on his shoulder, and told them all that she did indeed owe the supreme joy that had come to her to him. "No, Gavinia," she said, blushing, "I will not give you the particulars, but I assure you that had it not been for Tommy, Mr. McLean would never have asked me to marry him."

Elspeth crossed proudly to the side of her noble brother (who could scarcely trust his ears), and Gavinia cried in wonder, "What did he do?"

Now McLean had seen Tommy's tears also, and being a kindly man he dropped the satirist and chimed in warmly, "And if I had not asked Miss Ailie to marry me I should have lost the great happiness of my life, so you may all imagine how beholden I feel to Tommy."

Again Tommy was the centre-piece, and though these words were as puzzling to him as to his crew, their sincerity was unmistakable, and once more his head began to waggle complacently.

"And to show how grateful we are," said Miss Ailie, "we are to give him a—a sort of marriage present. We are to double the value of the bursary he wins at the university—" She could get no further, for now Elspeth was hugging her, and Corp cheering frantically, and Mr. McLean thought it necessary to add the warning, "If he does carry a bursary, you understand; for, should he fail, I give him nothing."

"Him fail!" exclaimed Corp, with whom Miss Ailie of course agreed. "And he can spend the money in whatever way he chooses," she said. "What will you do with it, Tommy?"

The lucky boy answered instantly, "I'll take Elspeth to Aberdeen to bide with me," and then Elspeth hugged him, and Miss Ailie said in a delighted aside to Mr. McLean, "I told you so," and he, too, was well pleased.

"It was the one thing needed to make him work," the schoolmistress whispered. "Is not his love for his sister beautiful?"

McLean admitted that it was, but half-banteringly he said to Elspeth: "What could you do in lodgings, you excited mite?"

"I can sit and look at Tommy," she answered quickly.

"But he will be away for hours at his classes."

"I'll sit at the window waiting for him," said she.

"And I'll run back quick," said Tommy.

All this time another problem had been bewildering Gavinia, and now she broke in eagerly: "But what was it he did? I thought he was agin Mr. McLean."

"And so did I," said Corp.

"I cheated you grandly," replied Tommy, with the audacity he found so useful.

"And a' the time you was pretending to be agin him," screamed Gavinia, "was you—was you bringing this about on the sly?"

Tommy looked up into Mr. McLean's face, but could get no guidance from it, so he said nothing: he only held his head higher than ever. "Oh, the clever little curse!" cried Corp, and Elspeth's delight was as ecstatic, though differently worded. Yet Gavinia stuck to her problem, "How did you do it, what was it you did?" and the cruel McLean said: "You may tell her, Tommy; you have my permission."

It would have been an awkward position for most boys, and even Tommy—but next moment he said quite coolly: "I think you and me and Miss Ailie should keep it to oursel's, Gavinia's sic a gossip."

"Oh, how thoughtful of him!" cried Miss Ailie the deceived, and McLean said: "How very thoughtful!" but now he saw in a flash why Mr.

Cathro still had hopes that Tommy might carry a bursary.

Thus was the repentant McLean pardoned, and nothing remained for him to do save to show the crew his Lair, which they had sworn to destroy. He had behaved so splendidly that they had forgotten almost that they were the emissaries of justice; but not to destroy the Lair seemed a pity, it would be such a striking way of bringing their adventures in the Den to a close. The degenerate Stuart read this feeling in their faces, and he was ready, he said, to show them his Lair if they would first point it out to him; but here was a difficulty, for how could they do that? For a moment it seemed as if the negotiations must fall through; but Sandys, that captain of resource, invited McLean to step aside for a private conference, and when they rejoined the others, McLean said gravely that he now remembered where the Lair was and would guide them to it.

They had only to cross a plank, invisible in the mist until they were close to it, and climb a slippery bank strewn with fallen trees. McLean, with a mock serious air, led the way, Miss Ailie on his arm. Corp and Gavinia followed, weighted and hampered by their new half-crowns, and Tommy and Elspeth in the rear whispered joyously of the coming life. And so, very unprepared for it, they moved toward the tragedy of the night.

CHAPTER XXXI

"Do you keep a light burning in the Lair?"
McLean turned to ask, forgetting for the moment
that it was not their domicile, but his.

"No, there's no light," replied Corp, equally
forgetful; but even as he spoke, he stopped so
suddenly that Elspeth struck against him. For
he had seen a light. "This is queer!" he cried,
and both he and Gavinia fell back in consterna-
tion. McLean pushed forward alone, and was
back in a trice, with a new expression on his face.
"Are you playing some trick on me?" he demanded suspiciously of Tommy. "There is
some one there; I almost ran against a pair of
blazing eyes."

"But there's nobody; there can be nobody
there," answered Tommy in a bewilderment that
was obviously unfeigned, "unless—unless——"
He looked at Corp, and the eyes of both finished the
sentence. The desolate scene at Double Dykes,
which the meeting with McLean and Miss Ailie
had driven from their minds, again confronted

391

them, and they seemed once more to hear the whimpering of the Painted Lady's door.

"Unless what?" asked the man impatiently. But still the two boys only stared at each other. "The Den's no mous the night," said Corp at last in a low voice, and his unspoken fears spread to the womankind, so that Miss Ailie shuddered and Elspeth gripped Tommy with both hands and Gavinia whispered, "Let's away hame, we can come back in the daylight."

But McLean chafed and pressed upward, and next moment a girl's voice was heard crying: "It is no business of yours; I won't let you touch her."

"Grizel!" exclaimed Tommy and his crew simultaneously, and they had no more fear until they were inside the Lair. What they saw had best be described very briefly. A fire was burning in a corner of the Lair, and in front of it, partly covered with a sheet, lay the Painted Lady dead. Grizel stood beside the body guarding it, her hands clenched, her eyes very strange. "You sha'n't touch her!" she cried passionately, and repeated it many times, as if she had lost the power to leave off, but Corp crept past her and raised the coverlet.

"She's straikit!" he shouted. "Did you do it yoursel', Grizel? God behears, she did it hersel'!"

A very long silence it seemed to be after that.

392

Miss Ailie would have taken the motherless girl to her arms, but first, at Corp's discovery, she had drawn back in uncontrollable repulsion, and Grizel, about to go to her, saw it, and turned from her to Tommy. Her eyes rested on him beseechingly, with a look he saw only once again in them until she was a woman; but his first thought was not for Grizel. Elspeth was clinging to him, terrified and sobbing, and he cried to her, "Shut your een," and then led her tenderly away. He was always good to Elspeth.

There was no lack of sympathy with Grizel when the news spread through the town, and un-shod men with their gallowses hanging down and women buttoning as they ran, hurried to the Den. But to all the questions put to her and to all the kindly offers made, as the body was carried to Double Dykes, she only rocked her arms, crying, "I don't want anything to eat. I shall stay all night beside her. I am not frightened at my mamma. I won't tell you why she was in the Den. I am not sure how long she has been dead. Oh, what do these little things matter?"

The great thing was that her mamma should be buried in the cemetery, and not in unconsecrated ground with a stake through her as the boys had predicted; and it was only after she was promised this, that Grizel told her little tale. She had feared for a long time that her mamma was dying of consumption, but she told no one, because everybody was against her and her mamma. Her mamma never knew that she was dying, and sometimes she used to get so much better that Grizel hoped she would live a long time, but that hope never lasted long. The reason she sat so much with Ballingall was just to find out what doctors did to dying people to make them live a little longer, and she watched his straiking to be able to do it to her mamma when the time came. She was sure none of the women would consent to straik her mamma. On the previous night, she could not say at what hour, she had been awakened by a cold wind, and so she knew that the door was open. She put out her hand in the darkness and found that her mamma was not beside her. It had happened before, and she was not frightened. She had hidden the key of the door that night and nailed down the window, but her mamma had found the key. Grizel rose, lit the lamp, and having dressed hurriedly, set off with wraps to the Den. Her mamma was generally as sensible as anybody in Thrums, but sometimes she had shaking fits, and after them she thought it was the time of long ago. Then she went to the Den to meet a man who had promised, she said, to be there, but he never came, and before daybreak Grizel could usually induce her to return home. Latterly she had persuaded her mamma to wait for him in the old Lair, because it was less cold there, and she had got her to do this last night. Her mamma did not seem very unwell, but she fell asleep, and she died sleeping, and then Grizel went back to Double Dykes for linen and straiked her.

Some say in Thrums that a spade was found in the Lair, but that is only the growth of later years. Grizel had done all she could do, and through the long Saturday she sat by the side of the body, helpless and unable to cry. She knew that it could not remain there much longer, but every time she rose to go and confess, fear of the indignities to which the body of her darling mamma might be subjected pulled her back. The boys had spoken idly; but hunted Grizel, who knew so much less and so much more than any of them, believed it all.

It was she who had stood so near Gavinia in the ruined house. She had only gone there to listen to human voices. When she discovered from the talk of her friends that she had left a light burning at Double Dykes and the door open, fear of the suspicions this might give rise to had sent her to the house on the heels of the two boys, and it was she who had stolen past them in the mist to put out the light and lock the door. Then she had returned to her mamma's side.

The doctor was among the listeners, almost the

only dry-eyed one, but he was not dry-eyed because he felt the artless story least. Again and again he rose from his chair restlessly, and Grizel thought he scowled at her when he was really scowling at himself; as soon as she had finished he cleared the room brusquely of all intruders, and then he turned on her passionately.

"Think shame of yoursel'," he thundered, "for keeping me in the dark," and of course she took his words literally, though their full meaning was, "I shall scorn myself from this hour for not having won the poor child's confidence."

Oh, he was a hard man, Grizel thought, the hardest of them all. But she was used to standing up to hard men, and she answered defiantly: "I did mean to tell you; that day you sent me with the bottle to Ballingall, I was waiting at the surgery door to tell you, but you were cruel, you said I was a thief, and then how could I tell you?"

This, too, struck home, and the doctor winced, but what he said was, "You fooled me for a whole week, and the town knows it; do you think I can forgive you for that?"

"I don't care whether you forgive me," replied Grizel at once.

"Nor do I care whether you care," he rapped out, all the time wishing he could strike himself; "but I'm the doctor of this place, and when your mother was ill you should have come straight to me. What had I done that you should be afraid of me?"

"I am not afraid of you," she replied, "I am not afraid of anyone, but mamma was afraid of you because she knew you had said cruel things about her, and I thought — I won't tell you what I thought." But with a little pressing she changed her mind and told him. "I was not sure whether you would come to see her, though I asked you; and if you came, I knew you would tell her she was dying, and that would have made her scream. And that is not all. I thought you might tell her that she would be buried with a stake through her ——"

"Oh, these blackguard laddies!" cried Mc-Queen, clenching his fists.

"And so I dared not tell you," Grizel concluded calmly; "I am not frightened at you, but I was frightened you would hurt my dear darling mamma," and she went and stood defiantly between him and her mother.

The doctor moved up and down the room, crying: "How did I not know of this, why was I not told?" and he knew that the fault had been his own, and so was furious when Grizel told him so.

"Yes, it is," she insisted, "you knew mamma was an unhappy lady, and that the people shouted things against her and terrified her; and you must have known, for everybody knew, that she was sometimes silly and wandered about all night, and you are a big strong man, and so you should have been sorry for her; and if you had been sorry, you would have come to see her and been kind to her, and then you would have found it all out."

"Have done, lassie!" he said, half angrily, half beseechingly; but she did not understand that he was suffering, and she went on relentlessly: "And you knew that bad men used to come to see her at night — they have not come for a long time — but you never tried to stop their coming, and I could have stopped it if I had known they were bad; but I did not know at first, and I was only a little girl, and you should have told me."

"Have done!" It was all that he could say, for, like many, he had heard of men visiting the Painted Lady by stealth, and he had only wondered, with other gossips, who they were.

He crossed again to the side of the dead woman. "And Ballingall's was the only corpse you ever saw straiked?" he said in wonder, she had done her work so well. But he was not doubting her; he knew already that this girl was clothed in truthfulness.

"Was it you that kept this house so clean?" he asked almost irritably, for he himself was the one undusted, neglected-looking thing in it, and he was suddenly conscious of his frayed wristband and of buttons hanging by a thread.

398

" Yes."

" What age are you ? "

" I think I am thirteen."

He looked long at her, vindictively she thought, but he was only picturing the probable future of a painted lady's child, and he said mournfully to himself, " Ay, it does not even end here ; and that's the crowning pity of it." But Grizel only heard him say, " Poor thing ! " and she bridled immediately.

" I won't let you pity me," she cried.

" You dour brat ! " he retorted. " But you need not think you are to have everything your own way still. I must get some Monypenny woman to take you till the funeral is over, and after that —— "

" I won't go," said Grizel, determinedly; " I shall stay with mamma till she is buried."

He was not accustomed to contradiction, and he stamped his foot. " You shall do as you are told," he said.

" I won't ! " replied Grizel, and she also stamped her foot.

" Very well, then, you thrawn tid; but at any rate I'll send in a woman to sleep with you."

" I want no one. Do you think I am afraid ? "

" I think you will be afraid when you wake up in the darkness and find yourself alone with — it."

" I sha'n't; I shall remember at once that she is

to be buried nicely in the cemetery, and that will make me happy."

"You unnatural —— "

"Besides, I sha'n't sleep; I have something to do."

His curiosity again got the better of the doctor. "What can you have to do at such a time?" he demanded, and her reply surprised him, "I am to make a dress."

"You!"

"I have made them before now," she said indignantly.

"But at such a time!"

"It is a black dress," she cried; "I don't have one. I am to make it out of mamma's."

He said nothing for some time, then "When did you think of this?"

"I thought of it weeks ago, I bought crape at the corner shop to be ready and —— "

She thought he was looking at her in horror, and stopped abruptly. "I don't care what you think," she said.

"What I do think," he retorted, taking up his hat, "is, that you are a most exasperating lassie. If I bide here another minute, I believe you'll get round me."

"I don't want to get round you."

"Then what makes you say such things? I question if I'll get an hour's sleep to-night for thinking of you."

"I don't want you to think of me!"

He groaned. "What could an untidy, hardened old single man like me do with you in his house?" he said. "Oh, you little limmer, to put such a thought into my head."

"I never did!" she exclaimed indignantly.

"It began, I do believe it began," he sighed, "the first time I saw you easing Ballingall's pillows."

"What began?"

"You brat, you wilful brat, don't pretend ignorance. You set a trap to catch me and ——"

"Oh!" cried Grizel, and she opened the door quickly. "Go away, you horrid man," she said.

He liked her the more for this regal action, and therefore it enraged him. Sheer anxiety lest he should succumb to her on the spot was what made him bluster as he strode off, and "That brat of a Grizel," or "The Painted Lady's most unbearable lassie," or "The dour little besom" was his way of referring to her in company for days; but if anyone agreed with him he roared, "Don't be a fool, man; she's a wonder, she's a delight," or "You have a dozen yourself, Janet, but I wouldna neifer Grizel for the lot of them." And it was he, still denouncing her so long as he was contradicted, who persuaded the Auld Licht Minister to officiate at the funeral. Then he said to himself, "And now I wash my hands of her; I have done all that can be expected of me." He told himself this a great many times, as if it were a medicine that must be taken frequently; and Grizel heard from Tommy, with whom she had some strange conversations, that he was going about denouncing her "up hill and down dale." But she did not care, she was so — so happy.

For a hole was dug for the Painted Lady in the cemetery, just as if she had been a good woman, and Mr. Dishart conducted the service in Double Dykes before the removal of the body, nor did he say one word that could hurt Grizel, perhaps because his wife had drawn a promise from him. A large gathering of men followed the coffin, three of them because, as you may remember, Grizel had dared them to stay away, but all the others out of sympathy with a motherless child who, as the procession started, rocked her arms in delight because her mamma was being buried respectably.

Being a woman, she could not attend the funeral, and so the chief mourner was Tommy, as you could see by the position he took at the grave and by the white bands Grizel had sewn on his sleeves. He was looking very important, as if he had something remarkable in prospect; but little attention was given him until the cords were dropped into the grave, and a prayer offered up, when he pulled Mr. Dishart's coat and muttered something about a paper. Those who had been making ready to depart swung round again, and the minister told him if he had anything to say to speak out.

"It's a paper," Tommy said, nervous yet elated, and addressing all, "that Grizel put in the coffin. She told me to tell you about it when the cords fell on the lid."

"What sort of a paper?" asked Mr. Dishart, frowning.

"It's — it's a letter to God," Tommy gasped.

Nothing was to be heard except the shoveling of earth into the grave. "Hold your spade, John," the minister said to the grave-digger, and then even that sound stopped. "Go on," Mr. Dishart signed to the boy.

"Grizel doesna believe her mother has much chance of getting to heaven," Tommy said, " and she wrote the letter to God, so that when He opens the coffins on the last day He will find it and read about them."

"About whom?" asked the stern minister.

"About Grizel's father, for one. She doesna know his name, but the Painted Lady wore a locket wi' a picture of him on her breast, and it's buried wi' her, and Grizel told God to look at it so as to know him. She thinks her mother will be damned for having her, and that it winna be fair unless God damns her father too."

"Go on," said Mr. Dishart.

"There was three Thrums men — I think they

were gentlemen," Tommy continued almost blithely, "that used to visit the Painted Lady in the night-time, afore she took ill. They wanted Grizel to promise no to tell about their going to Double Dykes, and she promised because she was ower innocent to know what they went for — but their names are in the letter."

A movement in the crowd was checked by the minister's uplifted arm. "Go on," he cried.

"She wouldna tell me who they were, because it would have been breaking her promise," said Tommy, "but — " he looked around him inquisitively — "but they're here at the funeral."

The mourners were looking sideways at each other, some breathing hard, but none dared to speak before the minister. He stood for a long time in doubt, but at last he signed to John to proceed with the filling-in of the grave. Contrary to custom, all remained. Not until the grave was again level with the sward did Mr. Dishart speak, and then it was with a gesture that appalled his hearers. "This grave," he said, raising his arm, " is locked till the day of judgment."

Leaving him standing there, a threatening figure, they broke into groups and dispersed, walking slowly at first, and then fast, to tell their wives.

CHAPTER XXXII

AN ELOPEMENT

THE solitary child remained at Double Dykes, awaiting the arrival of her father, for the Painted Lady's manner of leaving the world had made such a stir that the neighbours said he must have heard of it, even though he were in London, and if he had the heart of a stone he could not desert his bairn. They argued thus among themselves, less as people who were sure of it than to escape the perplexing question, what to do with Grizel if the man never claimed her ? and before her they spoke of his coming as a certainty, because it would be so obviously the best thing for her. In the meantime they overwhelmed her with offers of everything she could need, which was kindly, but not essential, for after the funeral expenses had been paid (Grizel insisted on paying them herself) she had still several gold pieces, found in her mamma's beautiful tortoise-shell purse, and there were nearly twenty pounds in the bank.

But day after day passed, and the man had not come. Perhaps he resented the Painted Lady's ostentatious death; which, if he was nicely strung, must have jarred upon his nerves. He could hardly have acknowledged Grizel now without publicity being given to his private concerns. Or he may never have heard of the Painted Lady's death; or if he read it, he may not have known which painted lady in particular she was. Or he may have married, and told his wife all and she had forgiven him, which somehow, according to the plays and the novels, cuts the past adrift from a man and enables him to begin again at yesterday. Whatever the reason, Grizel's father was in no hurry to reveal himself; and, though not to her, among themselves the people talked of the probability of his not coming at all. She could not remain alone at Double Dykes, they all admitted; but where, then, should she go? No fine lady in need of a handmaid seemed to think a painted lady's child would suit; indeed, Grizel at first sight had not the manner that attracts philanthropists. Once only did the problem approach solution; a woman in the Denhead was willing to take the child because (she expressed it) as she had seven she might as well have eight, but her man said no, he would not have his bairns fil't. Others would have taken her cordially for a few weeks or months, had they not known that at the end of this time they would be blamed, even by themselves, if they let her go. All, in short, were eager to show her kindness if one would give her a home, but where was that one to be found?

Much of this talk came to Grizel through Tommy, and she told him in the house of Double Dykes that people need not trouble themselves about her, for she had no wish to stay with them. It was only charity they brought her; no one wanted her for herself. "It is because I am a child of shame," she told him dry-eyed.

He fidgeted on his chair, and asked, "What's that?" not very honestly.

"I don't know," she said, "no one will tell me, but it is something you can't love."

"You have a terrible wish to be loved," he said in wonder, and she nodded her head wistfully. "That is not what I wish for most of all, though," she told him; and when he asked what she wished for most of all, she said, "To love somebody — oh, it would be sweet!"

To Tommy, most sympathetic of mortals, she seemed a very pathetic little figure, and tears came to his eyes as he surveyed her; he could always cry very easily. "If it wasna for Elspeth," he began, stammering, "I could love you, but you winna let a body do onything on the sly."

It was a vague offer, but she understood, and became the old Grizel at once. "I don't want you to love me," she said indignantly; "I don't think you know how to love."

" Neither can you know, then," retorted Tommy huffily, " for there's nobody for you to love."

" Yes, there is," she said, " and I do love her and she loves me."

" But wha is she ? "

" That girl." To his amazement she pointed to her own reflection in the famous mirror the size of which had scandalised Thrums. Tommy thought this affection for herself barely respectable, but he dared not say so, lest he should be put to the door. " I love her ever so much," Grizel went on, " and she is so fond of me she hates to see me unhappy. Don't look so sad, dearest, darlingest," she cried vehemently ; " I love you, you know, oh, you sweet ! " and with each epithet she kissed her re- flection and looked defiantly at the boy.

" But you canna put your arms round her and hug her," he pointed out triumphantly, and so he had the last word after all. Unfortunately Grizel kept this side of her, new even to Tommy, hidden from all others, and her unresponsiveness lost her many possible friends. Even Miss Ailie, who now had a dressmaker in the blue-and-white room, sit- ting on a bedroom chair and sewing for her life (oh, the agony — or is it the rapture ? of having to decide whether to marry in gray with beads or brown plain to the throat), even sympathetic Miss Ailie, having met with several rebuffs, said that Grizel had a most unaffectionate nature, and, " Ay, she's hardy," agreed the town, "but it's better, maybe, for hersel'." There are none so unpopular as the silent ones.

If only Miss Ailie, or others like her, could have slipped noiselessly into Double Dykes at night, they would have found Grizel's pillow wet. But she would have heard them long before they reached the door, and jumped to the floor in terror, thinking it was her father's step at last. For, unknown to anyone, his coming, which the town so anxiously desired, was her one dread. She had told Tommy what she should say to him if he came, and Tommy had been awed and delighted, they were such scathing things; probably, had the necessity arisen, she would have found courage to say them, but they were made up in the daytime, and at night they brought less comfort. Then she listened fearfully and longed for the morning, wild ideas coursing through her head of flying before he could seize her; but when morning came, it brought other thoughts, as of the strange remarks she had heard about her mamma and herself during the past few days. To brood over these was the most unhealthy occupation she could find, but it was her only birthright. Many of the remarks came unguardedly from lips that had no desire to cause her pain, others fell in a rage because she would not tell what were the names in her letter to God. The words that troubled her most, perhaps, were the doctor's, "She is a brave lass, but it must be in her blood." They were not intended for her ears, but she heard. "What did he mean?" she asked Miss Ailie, Mrs. Dishart, and others who came to see her, and they replied with pain that it had only been a doctor's remark, of no importance to people who were well. "Then why are you crying?" she demanded, looking them full in the face with eyes there was no deceiving.

"Oh, why is everyone afraid to tell me the truth!" she would cry, beating her palms in anguish.

She walked into McQueen's surgery and said, "Could you not cut it out?" so abruptly that he wondered what she was speaking about.

"The bad thing that is in my blood," she explained. "Do cut it out; I sha'n't scream. I promise not to scream."

He sighed and answered, "If it could be cut out, lassie, I would try to do it, though it was the most dangerous of operations."

She looked in anguish at him. "There are cleverer doctors than you, aren't there?" she asked, and he was not offended.

"Ay, a hantle cleverer," he told her, "but none so clever as that. God help you, bairn, if you have to do it yourself some day."

"Can I do it myself?" she cried, brightening. "I shall do it now. Is it done with a knife?"

"With a sharper knife than a surgeon's," he answered, and then regretting he had said so much, he tried to cheer her. But that he could not do. "You are afraid to tell me the truth too," she said, and when she went away he was sorry for her, but not so sorry as she was for herself. "When I am grown up," she announced dolefully to Tommy, "I shall be a bad woman, just like mamma."

"Not if you try to be good," he said.

"Yes, I shall. There is something in my blood that will make me bad, and I so wanted to be good. Oh! oh! oh!"

She told him of the things she had heard people say, but though they perplexed him almost as much as her, he was not so hopeless of learning their meaning, for here was just the kind of difficulty he liked to overcome. "I'll get it out o' Blinder," he said with confidence in his ingenuity, "and then I'll tell you what he says." But however much he might strive to do so, Tommy could never repeat anything without giving it frills and other adornment of his own making, and Grizel knew this. "I must hear what he says myself," she insisted.

"But he winna speak plain afore you."

"Yes, he will, if he does not know I am there."

The plot succeeded, though only partially, for so quick was the blind man's sense of hearing that in the middle of the conversation he said sharply,

"Somebody's ahint the dyke!" and he caught Grizel by the shoulder. "It's the Painted Lady's lassie," he said when she screamed, and he stormed against Tommy for taking such advantage of his blindness. But to her he said gently, "I daresay you egged him on to this, meaning well, but you maun forget most of what I've said, especially about being in the blood. I spoke in haste, it doesna apply to the like of you."

"Yes, it does," replied Grizel, and all that had been revealed to her she carried hot to the surgery, Tommy stopping at the door in as great perturbation as herself. "I know what being in the blood is now," she said tragically to McQueen, "there is something about it in the Bible. I am the child of evil passions, and that means that I was born with wickedness in my blood. It is lying sleeping in me just now because I am only thirteen, and if I can prevent its waking when I am grown up I shall always be good, but a very little thing will waken it; it wants so much to be wakened, and if it is once wakened it will run all through me, and soon I shall be like mamma."

It was all horribly clear to her, and she would not wait for words of comfort that could only obscure the truth. Accompanied by Tommy, who said nothing, but often glanced at her, fascinated yet alarmed, as if expecting to see the ghastly change come over her at any moment — for he

was as convinced as she, and had the livelier imagination — she returned to Monypenny to beg of
Blinder to tell her one thing more. And he told
her, not speaking lightly, but because his words
contained a solemn warning to a girl who he
thought might need it.

" What sort of thing would be likeliest to waken
the wickedness ? " she asked, holding her breath
for the answer.

" Keeping company wi' ill men," said Blinder,
gravely.

" Like the man who made mamma wicked, like
my father ? "

" Ay," Blinder replied ; " fly from the like of him,
my lass, though it should be to the other end of
the world."

She stood quite still, with a most sorrowful face,
and then ran away, ran so swiftly that when Tommy, who had lingered for a moment, came to the
door she was already out of sight. Scarcely less
excited than she, he set off for Double Dykes, his
imagination in such a blaze that he looked fearfully in the pools of the burn for a black frock.
But Grizel had not drowned herself; she was standing erect in her home, like one at bay, her arms
rigid, her hands clenched, and when he pushed
open the door she screamed.

"Grizel," said the distressed boy, " did you
think I was him come for you ? "

"Yes!"

"Maybe he'll no come. The folk think he winna come."

"But if he does, if he does!"

"Maybe you needna go wi' him unless you're willing?"

"I must, he can compel me because he is my father. Oh! oh! oh!" She lay down on the bed, and on her eyes there slowly formed the little wells of water Tommy was to know so well in time. He stood by her side in anguish; for though his own tears came at the first call, he could never face them in others.

"Grizel," he said impulsively, "there's just one thing for you to do. You have money, and you maun run away afore he comes!"

She jumped up at that. "I have thought of it," she answered, "I am always thinking about it, but how can I — oh, how can I? It would not be respectable."

"To run away?"

"To go by myself," said the poor girl, "and I do want to be respectable, it would be sweet."

In some ways Tommy was as innocent as she, and her reasoning seemed to him to be sound. She was looking at him woefully, and entreaty was on her face; all at once he felt what a lonely little crittur she was, and in a burst of manhood —

But, "Dinna prig wi' me to go with you," he said, struggling.

"I have not!" she answered panting; and she had not in words, but the mute appeal was still on her face. "Grizel," he cried, "I'll come!"

Then she seized his hand and pressed it to her breast, saying, "Oh, Tommy, I am so fond of you!"

It was the first time she had admitted it, and his head wagged well content, as if saying for him, "I knew you would understand me some day." But next moment the haunting shadow that so often overtook him in the act of soaring fell cold upon his mind, and "I maun take Elspeth!" he announced, as if Elspeth had him by the leg.

"You sha'n't!" said Grizel's face.

"She winna let go," said Tommy's.

Grizel quivered from top to toe. "I hate Elspeth!" she cried, with curious passion, and the more moral Tommy was ashamed of her.

"You dinna ken how fond o' her I am," he said.

"Yes, I do."

"Then you shouldna want me to leave her and go wi' you."

"That is why I want it," Grizel blurted out, and now we are all ashamed of her. But fortunately Tommy did not see how much she had admitted in that hasty cry; and as neither would give way to the other, they parted stiffly, his last words being, "Mind, it wouldna be respectable to go by yoursel'," and hers "I don't care, I'm going." Nevertheless it was she who slept easily that night, and he who tossed about almost until cockcrow. She had only one ugly dream, of herself wandering from door to door in a strange town, asking for lodgings, but the woman who answered her weary knocks—there were many doors, but invariably the same woman—always asked suspiciously "Is Tommy with you?" and Grizel shook her head, and then the woman drove her away, perceiving that she was not respectable. This woke her, and she feared the dream would come true, but she clenched her fists in the darkness, saying, "I can't help it, I am going, and I won't have Elspeth," and after that she slept in peace. In the meantime Tommy, the imaginative — but that night he was not Tommy, rather was he Grizel, for he saw her as we can only see ourselves. Now she — or he, if you will — had been caught by her father and brought back, and she turned into a painted thing like her mother. She brandished a brandy bottle and a stream of foul words ran lightly from her mouth, and suddenly stopped, because she was wailing, "I wanted so to be good, it is sweet to be good!" Now a man with a beard was whipping her, and Tommy felt each lash on his own body, so that he had to strike out, and he started up in bed, and the horrible thing was that he had never been asleep. Thus it went on until early morning, when his eyes were red and his body was damp with sweat.

But now again he was Tommy, and at first even to think of leaving Elspeth was absurd. Yet it would be pleasant to leave Aaron, who disliked him so much. To disappear without a word would be a fine revenge, for the people would say that Aaron must have ill-treated him; and while they searched the pools of the burn for his body, Aaron would be looking on trembling, perhaps with a policeman's hand on his shoulder. Tommy saw the commotion as vividly as if the searchers were already out and he in a tree looking down at them; but in a second he also heard Elspeth skirling, and down he flung himself from the tree, crying, " I'm here, Elspeth, dinna greet; oh, what a brute I've been!" No, he could not leave Elspeth. How wicked of Grizel to expect it of him! She was a bad one, Grizel.

But having now decided not to go, his sympathy with the girl who was to lose him returned in a rush, and before he went to school he besought her to — it amounted to this, to be more like himself; that is, he begged her to postpone her departure indefinitely, not to make up her mind until to-morrow — or the day after — or the day after that.

He produced reasons, as that she had only four pounds and some shillings now, while by-and-by she might get the Painted Lady's money, at present in the bank; also she ought to wait for the money that would come to her from the roup of the furniture. But Grizel waived all argument aside; secure in her four pounds and shillings she was determined to go to-night, for her father might be here to-morrow; she was going to London because it was so big that no one could ever find her there, and she would never, never write to Tommy to tell him how she fared, lest the letter put her father on her track. He implored her to write once, so that the money owing her might be forwarded, but even this bribe did not move her, and he set off for school most gloomily.

Cathro was specially aggravating that day, nagged him, said before the whole school that he was a numskull, even fell upon him with the tawse, and for no earthly reason except that Tommy would not bother his head with the *oratio obliqua*. If there is any kind of dominie more maddening than another, it is the one who will not leave you alone (ask any thoughtful boy). How wretched the lot of him whose life is cast among fools not capable of understanding him! what was that saying about entertaining angels unawares? London! Grizel had more than sufficient money to take two there, and once in London, a wonder such as himself was bound to do wondrous things. Now that he thought of it, to become a minister was abhorrent to him; to preach would be rather nice; oh, what things he would say (he began to make them up, and they were so grand that he almost wept), but to be good after the sermon was over, always to be good, (even when Elspeth was out of the way), never to think queer unsayable things, never to say Stroke, never, in short, to "find a way"—he was appalled. If it had not been for Elspeth ——

So even Elspeth did not need him. When he went home from school, thinking only of her, he found that she had gone to the Auld Licht manse to play with little Margaret. Very well, if such was her wish, he would go. Nobody wanted him except Grizel. Perhaps when news came from London of his greatness, they would think more of him. He would send a letter to Thrums, asking Mr. McLean to transfer his kindness to Elspeth. That would show them what a noble fellow he was. Elspeth would really benefit by his disappearance; he was running away for Elspeth's sake. And when he was great, which would be in a few years, he would come back for her.

But no, he——. The dash represents Tommy swithering once more, and he was at one or other end of the swither all day. When he acted sharply it was always on impulse, and as soon as the die was cast he was a philosopher with no regrets.

But when he had time to reflect, he jumped miserably back and forward. So when Grizel was ready to start, he did not know in the least what he meant to do.

She was to pass by the Cuttle Well, on her way to Tilliedrum, where she would get the London train, he had been told coldly, and he could be there at the time — if he liked. The time was seven o'clock in the evening on a week-day, when the lovers are not in the Den, and Tommy arrived first. When he stole through the small field that separates Monypenny from the Den, his decision was — but on reaching the Cuttle Well, its nearness to the uncanny Lair chilled his courage, and now he had only come to bid her good-bye. She was very late, and it suddenly struck him that she had already set off. "After getting me to promise to go wi' her!" he said to himself at once.

But Grizel came; she was only late because it had taken her such a long time to say good-bye to the girl in the glass. She was wearing her black dress and lustre jacket, and carried in a bundle the few treasures she was taking with her, and though she did not ask Tommy if he was coming, she cast a quick look round to see if he had a bundle anywhere, and he had none. That told her his decision, and she would have liked to sit down for a minute and cry, but of course she had too much pride, and she bade him farewell so promptly that he thought he had a grievance. "I'm coming as far as the toll-house wi' you," he said sulkily, and so they started together.

At the toll-house Grizel stopped. "It's a fine night," said Tommy almost apologetically, "I'll go as far as the quarry o' Benshee."

When they came to the quarry, he said, "We're no half-roads yet, I'll go wi' you as far as Padanarum." Now she began to wonder and to glance at him sideways, which made him more uncomfortable than ever. To prevent her asking him a question for which he had no answer, he said, "What makes you look so little the day?"

"I am not looking little," she replied, greatly annoyed, "I am looking taller than usual. I have let down my frock three inches so as to look taller — and older."

"You look younger than ever," he said cruelly.

"I don't! I look fifteen, and when you are fifteen you grow up very quickly. Do say I look older!" she entreated anxiously. "It would make me feel more respectable."

But he shook his head with surprising obstinacy, and then she began to remark on his clothes, which had been exercising her curiosity ever since they left the Den.

"How is it that you are looking so stout?" she asked. "I feel cold, but you are wiping the sweat off your face every minute."

It was true, but he would have preferred not to answer. Grizel's questions, however, were all so straight in the face that there was no dodging them. "I have on twa suits o' clothes, and a' my sarks," he had to admit, sticky and sullen.

She stopped, but he trudged on doggedly. She ran after him and gave his arm an impulsive squeeze with both hands. "Oh, you sweet!" she said.

"No, I'm not," he answered in alarm.

"Yes you are! You are coming with me."

"I'm not!"

"Then why did you put on so many clothes?"

Tommy swithered wretchedly on one foot. "I didna put them on to come wi' you," he explained, "I just put them on in case I should come wi' you."

"And you are not coming?"

"How can I ken?"

"But you must decide!" Grizel almost screamed.

"I needna," he stammered, "till we're at Tilliedrum. Let's speak about some other thing."

She rocked her arms, crying, "It is so easy to make up one's mind."

"It's easy to you that has just one mind," he retorted with spirit, "but if you had as many minds as I have ——!"

On they went.

CHAPTER XXXIII

THERE IS SOMEONE TO LOVE GRIZEL AT LAST

CORP was sitting on the Monypenny dyke, spitting on a candlestick and then rubbing it briskly against his orange-coloured trousers. The doctor passing in his gig, both of them streaked, till they blended, with the mud of Look-about-you road (through which you should drive winking rapidly all the way), saw him and drew up.

"Well, how is Grizel?" he asked. He had avoided Double Dykes since the funeral, but vain had been his attempts to turn its little inmate out of his mind; there she was, against his will, and there, he now admitted to himself angrily, or with a rueful sigh, she seemed likely to remain until someone gave her a home. It was an almost ludicrous distrust of himself that kept him away from her; he feared that if he went to Double Dykes her lonely face would complete his conquest. For — oh, he was reluctant to be got the better of, as he expressed it to himself. Maggy Ann, his maid, was the ideal woman for a bachelor's house. When she saw him coming she fled, guiltily concealing the hated duster; when he roared at her for announcing that dinner was ready, she left him to eat it half cold; when he spilled matches on the floor and then stepped upon them and set the rug on fire, she let him tell her that she should be more careful; she did not carry off his favourite boots to the cobbler because they were down at heel; she did not fling up her arms in horror and cry that she had brushed that coat just five minutes ago; nor did she count the treasured "dottels" on the mantelpiece to discover how many pipes he had smoked since morning; nor point out that he had stepped over the door-mat; nor line her shelves with the new *Mentor;* nor giving him up his foot for sitting half the night with patients who could not pay — in short, he knew the ways of the limmers, and Maggy Ann was a jewel. But it had taken him a dozen years to bring her to this perfection, and well he knew that the curse of Eve, as he called the rage for the duster, slumbered in her rather than was extinguished. With the volcanic Grizel in the house, Maggy Ann would once more burst into flame, and the horrified doctor looked to right of him, to left of him, before him and behind him, and everywhere he seemed to see two new brooms bearing down. No, the brat, he would not have her; the besom; why did she bother him; the witches take her, for putting the idea into his head, nailing it into his head, indeed! But nevertheless he was for ever urging other people to adopt her, assuring them that they would find her a treasure, and even shaking his staff at them when they refused; and he was so uneasy if he did not hear of her several times a day that he made Monypenny the way to and from everywhere, so that he might drop into artful talk with those who had seen her last. Corp, accordingly, was not surprised at his " How is Grizel ? " now, and he answered, between two spits, " She's fine ; she gave me this."

It was one of the Painted Lady's silver candlesticks, and the doctor asked sharply why Grizel had given it to him.

" She said because she liked me," Corp replied, wonderingly. " She brought it to my auntie's door soon after I loused, and put it into my hand; ay, and she had a blue shawl, and she telled me to give it to Gavinia, because she liked her too."

" What else did she say ? "

Corp tried to think. " I said, ' This cows, Grizel, but thank you kindly,' " he answered, much pleased with his effort of memory, but the doctor interrupted him rudely. " Nobody wants to hear what you said, you dottrel; what more did she say ? " And thus encouraged, Corp remembered that she had said she hoped he would not forget her. " What for should I forget her when I see her ilka day ? " he asked, and was probably about to divulge that this was his reply to her, but without waiting for more, McQueen turned his beast's head and drove to the entrance to the double dykes. Here he alighted and hastened up the path on foot, but before he reached the house he met Dite Deuchars taking his ease beneath a tree, and Dite could tell him that Grizel was not at home. " But there's somebody in Double Dykes," he said, " though I kenna wha could be there unless it's the ghost of the Painted Lady hersel'. About an hour syne I saw Grizel come out o' the house, carrying a bundle, but she hadna gone many yards when she turned round and waved her hand to the east window. I couldna see wha was at it, but there maun have been somebody, for first the crittur waved to the window and next she kissed her hand to it, and syne she went on a bit, and syne she ran back close to the window and nodded and flung more kisses, and back and forrit she went a curran times as if she could hardly tear hersel' awa'. ' Wha's that you're so chief wi' ? ' I speired when she came by me at last, but she just said, ' I won't tell you,' in her dour wy, and she hasna come back yet."

Whom could she have been saying good-bye to so demonstratively, and whither had she gone ? With a curiosity that for the moment took the place of his uneasiness, McQueen proceeded to the house, the door of which was shut but not locked.

Two glances convinced him that there was no one here; the kitchen was as he had seen it last, except that the long mirror had been placed on a chair close to the east window. The doctor went to the outside of the window and looked in; he could see nothing but his own reflection in the mirror, and was completely puzzled. But it was no time, he felt, for standing there scratching his head, when there was reason to fear that the girl had gone. Gone where? He saw his selfishness now, in a glaring light, and it fled out of him pursued by curses.

He stopped at Aaron's door and called for Tommy, but Tommy had left the house an hour ago. "Gone with her, the sacket; he very likely put her up to this," the doctor muttered, and the surmise seemed justified when he heard that Grizel and Tommy had been seen passing the Fens. That they were running away had never struck those who saw them, and McQueen said nothing of his suspicions, but off he went in his gig on their track and ran them down within a mile of Tilliedrum. Grizel scurried on, thinking it was undoubtedly her father, but in a few minutes the three were conversing almost amicably, the doctor's first words had been so "sweet."

Tommy explained that they were out for a walk, but Grizel could not lie, and in a few passionate sentences she told McQueen the truth. He had guessed the greater part of it, and while she spoke he looked so sorry for her, such a sweet change had come over his manner, that she held his hand.

" But you must go no farther," he told her, " I am to take you back with me," and that alarmed her. " I won't go back," she said determinedly, " he might come."

" There's little fear of his coming," McQueen assured her, gently, " but if he does come I give you my solemn word that I won't let him take you away unless you want to go."

Even then she only wavered, but he got her altogether with this : " And should he come, just think what a piece of your mind you could give him, with me standing by holding your hand."

" Oh, would you do that ? " she asked, brightening.

" I would do a good deal to get the chance," he said.

" I should just love it ! " she cried. " I shall come now," and she stepped light-heartedly into the gig, where the doctor joined her. Tommy, who had been in the background all this time, was about to jump up beside them, but McQueen waved him back, saying maliciously, " There's just room for two, my man, so I won't interfere with your walk."

Tommy, in danger of being left, very hot and

428

stout and sulky, whimpered, "What have I done to anger you?"

"You were going with her, you blackguard," replied McQueen, not yet in full possession of the facts, for whether Tommy was or was not going with her no one can ever know.

"If I was," cried the injured boy, "it wasna because I wanted to go, it was because it wouldna have been respectable for her to go by hersel'."

The doctor had already started his shalt, but at these astonishing words he drew up sharply. "Say that again," he said, as if thinking that his ears must have deceived him, and Tommy repeated his remark, wondering at its effect.

"And you tell me that you were going with her," the doctor repeated, "to make her enterprise more respectable?" and he looked from one to the other.

"Of course I was," replied Tommy, resenting his surprise at a thing so obvious; and "That's why I wanted him to come," chimed in Grizel.

Still McQueen's glance wandered from the boy to the girl, and from the girl to the boy. "You are a pair!" he said at last, and he signed in silence to Tommy to mount the gig. But his manner had alarmed Grizel, ever watching herself lest she should stray into the ways of bad ones, and she asked anxiously, "There was nothing wrong in it, was there?"

"No," the doctor answered gravely, laying his hand on hers, "no, it was just sweet."

What McQueen had to say to her was not for Tommy's ears, and the conversation was but a make-shift until they reached Thrums, where he sent the boy home, recommending him to hold his tongue about the escapade (and Tommy of course saw the advisability of keeping it from Elspeth); but he took Grizel into his parlour and set her down on the buffet stool by the fire, where he surveyed her in silence at his leisure. Then he tried her in his old armchair, then on his sofa; then he put the *Mentor* into her hand, and told her to hold it as if it were a duster, then he sent her into the passage, with in-structions to open the door presently and announce "Dinner is ready"; then he told her to put some coals on the fire; then he told her to sit at the win-dow, first with an open book in her hand, secondly as if she was busy knitting; and all these things she did wondering exceedingly, for he gave no explanation except the incomprehensible one, "I want to see what it would be like."

She had told him in the gig why she had changed the position of the mirror at Double Dykes; it was to let "that darling" wave good-bye to her from the window; and now having experimented with her in his parlour, he drew her toward his chair, so that she stood between his knees. And he asked her if she understood why he had gone to Double Dykes.

" Was it to get me to tell you what were the names in the letter? " she said wistfully. " That is what everyone asks me, but I won't tell — no, I won't; " and she closed her mouth hard.

He, too, would have liked to hear the names, and he sighed, it must be admitted, at sight of that determined mouth, but he could say truthfully, " Your refusal to break your promise is one of the things that I admire in you."

Admire! Grizel could scarce believe that this gift was for her. " You don't mean that you really like me? " she faltered, but she felt sure all the time that he did, and she cried, "Oh, but why? oh, how can you? "

" For one reason," he said, " because you are so good."

"Good! Oh! oh! oh!" She clapped her hands joyously.

" And, for another — because you are so brave."

" But I am not really brave," she said anxiously, yet resolved to hide nothing; " I only pretend to be brave; I am often frightened, but I just don't let on."

That, he told her, is the highest form of bravery, but Grizel was very, very tired of being brave, and she insisted impetuously, " I don't want to be brave, I want to be afraid, like other girls."

"Ay, it's your right, you little woman," he answered tenderly; and then again he became mysterious. He kicked off his shoes to show her that he was wearing socks that did not match. "I just pull on the first that come to hand," he said recklessly.

"Oh!" cried Grizel.

On his dusty book-shelves he wrote, with his finger, "Not dusted since the year One."

"Oh! oh!" she cried.

He put his fingers through his gray, untidy hair. "That's the only comb I have that is at hand when I want it," he went on, regardless of her agony.

"All the stud-holes in my shirts," he said, "are now so frayed and large that the studs fall out, and I find them in my socks at night."

Oh! oh! he was killing her, he was, but what cared he? "Look at my clothes," said the cruel man, "I read when I'm eating, and I spill so much gravy that — that we boil my waistcoat once a month, and make soup of it!"

To Grizel this was the most tragic picture ever drawn by man, and he saw that it was time to desist. "And it's all," he said, looking at her sadly, "it's all because I'm a lonely old bachelor with no womankind to look after him, no little girl to brighten him when he comes home dog-tired, no one to care whether his socks are in holes and his comb behind the wash-stand, no soft hand to soothe his brow when it aches, no one to work for, no one

432

to love, many a one to close the old bachelor's eyes when he dies, but none to drop a tear for him, no one to ———"

"Oh! oh! oh! That is just like me. Oh! oh!" cried Grizel, and he pulled her closer to him, saying, " The more reason we should join thegither; Grizel, if you don't take pity on me, and come and bide with me and be my little housekeeper, the Lord Almighty only knows what is to become of the old doctor."

At this she broke away from him, and stood far back pressing her arms to her sides, and she cried, " It is not out of charity you ask me, is it?" and then she went a little nearer. " You would not say it if it wasn't true, would you?"

" No, my dawtie, it's true," he told her, and if he had been pitying himself a little, there was an end of that now.

She remembered something and cried joyously, " And you knew what was in my blood before you asked me, so I don't need to tell you, do I? And you are not afraid that I shall corrupt you, are you? And you don't think it a pity I didn't die when I was a tiny baby, do you? Some people think so — I heard them say it."

" What would have become of me?" was all he dared answer in words, but he drew her to him again, and when she asked if it was true, as she had heard some woman say, that in some matters men were all alike and did what that one man had done to her mamma, he could reply solemnly, "No, it is not true; it's a lie that has done more harm than any war in any century."

She sat on his knee, telling him many things that had come recently to her knowledge but were not so new to him. The fall of woman was the subject — a strange topic for a girl of thirteen and a man of sixty. They don't become wicked in a moment, he learned; if they are good to begin with, it takes quite a long time to make them bad. Her mamma was good to begin with. "I know she was good, because when she thought she was the girl she used to be, she looked sweet and said lovely things. The way the men do is this: they put evil thoughts into the woman's head, and say them often to her, till she gets accustomed to them, and thinks they cannot be bad when the man she loves likes them, and it is called corrupting the mind.

"And then a baby comes to them," Grizel said softly, "and it is called a child of shame. I am a child of shame."

He made no reply, so she looked up, and his face was very old and sad. "I am sorry too," she whispered, but still he said nothing, and then she put her fingers on his eyes to discover if they were wet, and they were wet. And so Grizel knew that there was someone who loved her at last.

The mirror was the only article of value that Grizel took with her to her new home; everything else was rouped at the door of Double Dykes; Tommy, who should have been at his books, acting as auctioneer's clerk for sixpence. There are houses in Thrums where you may still be told who got the bed and who the rocking-chair, and how Nether Drumgley's wife dared him to come home without the spinet; but it is not by the sales that the roup is best remembered. Curiosity took many persons into Double Dykes that day, and in the room that had never been furnished they saw a mournful stack of empty brandy bottles, piled there by the auctioneer, who had found them in every corner, beneath the bed, in presses, in boxes, whither they had been thrust by Grizel's mamma, as if to conceal their number from herself. The counting of these bottles was a labour, but it is not even by them that the roup is remembered. Among them some sacrilegious hands found a bundle of papers with a sad blue ribbon round them. They were the Painted Lady's love-letters, the letters she had written to the man. Why or how they had come back to her no one knew.

Most of them were given to Grizel, but a dozen or more passed without her leave into the kists of various people, where often since then they have been consulted by swains in need of a pretty phrase; and Tommy's schoolfellows, the very boys and girls who hooted the Painted Lady, were in time — so oddly do things turn out — to be among those whom her letters taught how to woo. Where the kists did not let in the damp or careless fingers, the paper long remained clean, the ink but little faded. Some of the letters were creased, as if they had been much folded, perhaps for slipping into secret hiding-places, but none of them bore any address or a date. "To my beloved," was sometimes written on the cover, and inside he was darling or beloved again. So no one could have arranged them in the order in which they were written, though there was a three-cornered one which said it was the first. There was a violet in it, clinging to the paper as if they were fond of each other, and Grizel's mamma had written, "The violet is me, hiding in a corner because I am so happy." The letters were in many moods, playful, reflective, sad, despairing, arch, but all were written in an ecstasy of the purest love, and most of them were cheerful, so that you seemed to see the sun dancing on the paper while she wrote, the same sun that afterwards showed up her painted cheeks. Why they came back to her no one ever discovered, any more than how she who slipped the violet into that three-cornered one and took it out to kiss again and wrote, "It is my first love-letter, and I love it so much I am reluctant to let it go," became in a few years the derision of the

Double Dykes. Some of these letters may be in old kists still, but whether that is so or not, they alone have passed the Painted Lady's memory from one generation to another, and they have purified it, so that what she was died with her vile body, and what she might have been lived on, as if it were her true self.

CHAPTER XXXIV

MISS ALISON CRAY presents her compliments to
—— and requests the favour of their company at
her marriage with Mr. Ivie McLean, on January
8th, at six o'clock."

Tommy in his Sabbath clothes, with a rose from
the Dovecot hothouse for buttonhole (which he
slipped into his pocket when he saw other boys
approaching), delivered them at the doors of the
aristocracy, where, by the way, he had been a few
weeks earlier, with another circular:

" Miss Alison Cray, being about to give up
school, has pleasure in stating that she has dis-
posed of the goodwill of her establishment to Miss
Jessy Langlands and Miss S. Oram, who will enter
upon their scholastic duties on January 9th, at
Roods Cottage, where she most cordially," and
so on.

Here if the writer dared (but you would be so
angry) he would introduce at the length of a
chapter two brand-new characters, the Misses
Langlands and Oram, who suddenly present them-

438

selves to him in the most sympathetic light. Miss Ailie had been safely stowed to port, but their little boat is only setting sail, and they are such young ones, neither out of her teens, that he would fain turn for a time from her to them. Twelve pounds they paid for the goodwill, and, oh, the exciting discussions, oh, the scraping to get the money together! If little Miss Langlands had not been so bold, big Miss Oram must have drawn back, but if Miss Oram had not had that idea about a paper partition, of what avail the boldness of Miss Langlands? How these two trumps of girls succeeded in hiring the Painted Lady's spinet from Nether Drumgley — in the absence of his wife, who on her way home from buying a Cochin-china met the spinet in a cart — how the mother of one of them, realising in a klink that she was common no more, henceforth wore black caps instead of mutches (but the father dandered on in the old plebeian way); what the enterprise meant to a young man in distant Newcastle, whose favourite name was Jessy; how the news travelled to still more distant Canada, where a family of emigrants which had left its Sarah behind in Thrums, could talk of nothing else for weeks — it is hard to have to pass on without dwelling on these things, and indeed — but pass on we must.

The chief figure at the wedding of Miss Ailie was undoubtedly Mr. T. Sandys. When one remembers his prominence, it is difficult to think that the wedding could have taken place without him. It was he (in his Sabbath clothes again, and now flaunting his buttonhole brazenly) who in insulting language ordered the rabble to stand back there. It was he who dashed out to the 'Sosh to get a hundred ha'pennies for the fifty pennies Mr. McLean had brought to toss into the air. It was he who went round in the carriage to pick up the guests, and whisked them in and out, and slammed the door, and saw to it that the minister was not kept waiting, and warned Miss Ailie that if she did not come now they should begin without her. It was he who stood near her with a handkerchief ready in his hand lest she took to crying on her new brown silk (Miss Ailie was married in brown silk after all). As a crown to his audacity, it was he who told Mr. Dishart, in the middle of a noble passage, to mind the lamp.

These duties were Dr. McQueen's, the best man, but either demoralized by the bridegroom, who went all to pieces at the critical moment and was much more nervous than the bride, or in terror lest Grizel, who had sent him to the wedding speckless and most beautifully starched, should suddenly appear at the door and cry, " Oh, oh, take your fingers off your shirt ! " he was through other till the knot was tied, and then it was too late, for Tommy had made his mark. It was Tommy who led the way to the schoolroom where the feast was ready, it was Tommy who put the guests in their places (even the banker cringed to him), it was Tommy who winked to Mr. Dishart to say grace. As you will readily believe, Miss Ailie could not endure the thought of excluding her pupils from the festivities, and they began to arrive as soon as the tables had been cleared of all save oranges and tarts and raisins. Tommy, waving Gavinia aside, showed them in, and one of them, curious to tell, was Corp, in borrowed blacks, and Tommy shook hands with him and called him Mr. Shiach, both new experiences to Corp, who knocked over a table in his anxiety to behave himself, and roared at intervals " Do you see the little deevil! " and bit his warts and then politely swallowed the blood.

As if oranges and tarts and raisins were not enough, came the Punch and Judy show, Tommy's culminating triumph. All the way to Redlintie had Mr. McLean sent for the Punch and Judy show, and nevertheless there was a probability of no performance, for Miss Ailie considered the show immoral. Most anxious was she to give pleasure to her pupils, and this she knew was the best way, but how could she countenance an entertainment which was an encouragement to every form of vice and crime ? To send these children to the Misses Langlands and Oram, fresh from an introduction to the comic view of murder ! It could not be

done, now could it? Mr. McLean could make no
suggestion. Mr. Dishart thought it would be advisable to substitute another entertainment; was
there not a game called " The Minister's Cat " ?
Mrs. Dishart thought they should have the show
and risk the consequences. So also thought Dr.
McQueen. The banker was consulted, but saw no
way out of the difficulty, nor did the lawyer, nor
did the Misses Finlayson. Then Tommy appeared
on the scene, and presently retired to find a way.

He found it. The performance took place, and
none of the fun was omitted, yet neither Miss
Ailie — tuts, tuts, Mrs. McLean — nor Mr. Dishart
could disapprove. Punch did chuck his baby out
at the window (roars of laughter) in his jovial,
time-honoured way, *but* immediately thereafter up
popped the showman to say, " Ah, my dear boys
and girls, let this be a lesson to you never to destroy your offsprings. Oh, shame on Punch, for to
do the wicked deed; he will be catched in the end,
and serve him right." Then when Mr. Punch had
walloped his wife with the stick, amid thunders of
applause, up again bobbed the showman: " Ah,
my dear boys and girls, what a lesson is this we
sees, what goings on is this ? He have bashed the
head of her as should ha' been the apple of his eye,
and he does not care a — he does not care; but
mark my words, his home it will now be desolate,
no more shall she meet him at his door with kindly

smile, he have done for her quite, and now he is a hunted man. Oh, be warned by his sad igsample, and do not bash the head of your loving wife." And there was a great deal more of the same, and simple Mrs. McLean almost wept tears of joy because her favourite's good heart had suggested these improvements.

Grizel was not at the wedding; she was invited, but could not go because she was in mourning. But only her parramatty frock was in mourning, for already she had been the doctor's housekeeper for two full months, and her father had not appeared to plague her (he never did appear, it may be told at once), and so how could her face be woful when her heart leapt with gladness? Never had prisoner pined for the fields more than this reticent girl to be frank, and she poured out her inmost self to the doctor, so that daily he discovered something beautiful (and exasperating) about womanhood. And it was his love for her that had changed her. "You do love me, don't you?" she would say, and his answer might be, "I have told you that fifty times already;" to which she would reply gleefully, "That is not often, I say it all day to myself."

Exasperating? Yes, that was the word. Long before summer came, the doctor knew that he had given himself into the hands of a tyrant. It was idle his saying that this irregularity and that carelessness were habits that had become part of him; she only rocked her arms impatiently, and if he would not stand still to be put to rights, then she would follow him along the street, brushing him as he walked, a sight that was witnessed several times while he was in the mutinous stage.

"Talk about masterfulness," he would say, when she whipped off his coat or made a dart at the mud on his trousers; "you are the most masterful little besom I ever clapped eyes on."

But as he said it he perhaps crossed his legs, and she immediately cried, "You have missed two holes in lacing your boots!"

Of a morning he would ask her sarcastically to examine him from top to toe and see if he would do, and examine him she did, turning him round, pointing out that he had been sitting "again" on his tails, that oh, oh, he must have cut that buttonhole with his knife. He became most artful in hiding deficiencies from her, but her suspicions once roused would not sleep, and all subterfuge was vain. "Why have you buttoned your coat up tight to the throat to-day?" she would demand sternly.

"It is such a cold morning," he said.

"That is not the reason," she replied at once (she could see through broadcloth at a glance), "I believe you have on the old necktie again, and you promised to buy a new one."

"I always forget about it when I'm out," he said humbly, and next evening he found on his table a new tie, made by Grizel herself out of her mamma's rokelay.

It was related by one who had dropped in at the doctor's house unexpectedly, that he found Grizel making a new shirt, and forcing the doctor to try on the sleeves while they were still in the pin stage.

She soon knew his every want, and just as he was beginning to want it, there it was at his elbow. He realised what a study she had made of him when he heard her talking of his favourite dishes and his favourite seat, and his way of biting his underlip when in thought, and how hard he was on his left cuff. It had been one of his boasts that he had no favourite dishes, etc., but he saw now that he had been a slave to them for years without knowing it.

She discussed him with other mothers as if he were her little boy, and he denounced her for it. But all the time she was spoiling him. Formerly he had got on very well when nothing was in its place. Now he roared helplessly if he mislaid his razor.

He was determined to make a lady of her, which necessitated her being sent to school; she preferred hemming, baking, and rubbing things till they shone, and not both could have had their

way (which sounds fatal for the man), had they
not arranged a compromise, Grizel, for instance,
to study geography for an hour in the evening
with Miss Langlands (go to school in the daytime
she would not) so long as the doctor shaved every
morning, but if no shave no geography; the doctor to wipe his pen on the blot-sheet instead of on
the lining of his coat if she took three lessons a
week from Miss Oram on the spinet. How happy
and proud she was! Her glee was a constant
source of wonder to McQueen. Perhaps she put
on airs a little, her walk, said the critical, had become a strut; but how could she help that when
the new joyousness of living was dancing and
singing within her?

Had all her fears for the future rolled away like
clouds that leave no mark behind? The doctor
thought so at times, she so seldom spoke of them
to him; he did not see that when they came she
hid them from him because she had discovered
that they saddened him. And she had so little
time to brood, being convinced of the sinfulness
of sitting still, that if the clouds came suddenly,
they never stayed long save once, and then it was,
mayhap, as well. The thunderclap was caused
by Tommy, who brought it on unintentionally and
was almost as much scared by his handiwork as
Grizel herself. She and he had been very friendly
of late, partly because they shared with McQueen

the secret of the frustrated elopement, partly because they both thought that in that curious incident Tommy had behaved in a most disinterested and splendid way. Grizel had not been sure of it at first, but it had grown on Tommy, he had so thoroughly convinced himself of his intention to get into the train with her at Tilliedrum that her doubts were dispelled — easily dispelled, you say, but the truth must be told, Grizel was very anxious to be rid of them. And Tommy's were honest convictions, born full grown of a desire for happiness to all. Had Elspeth discovered how nearly he had deserted her, the same sentiment would have made him swear to her with tears that never should he have gone farther than Tilliedrum, and while he was persuading her he would have persuaded himself. Then again, when he met Grizel — well, to get him in doubt it would have been necessary to catch him on the way between these two girls.

So Tommy and Grizel were friends, and finding that it hurt the doctor to speak on a certain subject to him, Grizel gave her confidences to Tommy. She had a fear, which he shared on its being explained to him, that she might meet a man of the stamp of her father, and grow fond of him before she knew the kind he was, and as even Tommy could not suggest an infallible test which would lay them bare at the first glance, he consented to consult Blinder once more. He found the blind man by his fireside, very difficult to coax into words on the important topic, but Tommy's "You've said ower much no to tell a bit more," seemed to impress him, and he answered the question,—

"You said a woman should fly frae the like o' Grizel's father though it should be to the other end of the world, but how is she to ken that he's that kind?"

"She'll ken," Blinder answered after thinking it over, "if she likes him and fears him at one breath, and has a sort of secret dread that he's getting a power ower her that she canna resist."

These words were a flash of light on a neglected corner to Tommy. "Now I see, now I ken," he exclaimed, amazed; "now I ken what my mother meant! Blinder, is that no the kind of man that's called masterful?"

"It's what poor women find them and call them to their cost," said Blinder.

Tommy's excitement was prodigious. "Now I ken, now I see!" he cried, slapping his leg and stamping up and down the room.

"Sit down!" roared his host.

"I canna," retorted the boy. "Oh, to think o't, to think I came to speir that question at you, to think her and me has wondered what kind he was, and I kent a' the time!" Without staying

448

to tell Blinder what he was blethering about, he hurried off to Grizel, who was waiting for him in the Den, and to her he poured out his astonishing news.

"I ken all about them, I've kent since afore I came to Thrums, but though I generally say the prayer, I've forgot to think o' what it means." In a stampede of words he told her all he could remember of his mother's story as related to him on a grim night in London so long ago, and she listened eagerly. And when that was over, he repeated first his prayer and then Elspeth's, "O God, whatever is to be my fate, may I never be one of them that bow the knee to masterful man, and if I was born like that and canna help it, O take me up to heaven afore I'm fil't." Grizel repeated it after him until she had it by heart, and even as she said it a strange thing happened, for she began to draw back from Tommy, with a look of terror on her face.

"What makes you look at me like that?" he cried.

"I believe — I think — you are masterful," she gasped.

"Me!" he retorted indignantly.

"Now," she went on, waving him back, "now I know why I would not give in to you when you wanted me to be Stroke's wife. I was afraid you were masterful!"

"Was that it?" cried Tommy.

"Now," she proceeded, too excited to heed his interruptions, "now I know why I would not kiss your hand, now I know why I would not say I liked you. I was afraid of you, I——"

"Were you?" His eyes began to sparkle, and something very like rapture was pushing the indignation from his face. "Oh, Grizel, have I a power over you?"

"No, you have not," she cried passionately. "I was just frightened that you might have. Oh, oh, I know you now!"

"To think o't, to think o't!" he crowed, wagging his head, and then she clenched her fist, crying, "Oh, you wicked, you should cry with shame!"

But he had his answer ready, "It canna be my wite, for I never kent o't till you telled me. Grizel, it has just come about without either of us kenning!"

She shuddered at this, and then seized him by the shoulders. "It has not come about at all," she said, "I was only frightened that it might come, and now it can't come, for I won't let it."

"But can you help yoursel'?"

"Yes, I can. I shall never be friends with you again."

She had such a capacity for keeping her word that this alarmed him, and he did his best to extinguish his lights. "I'm no masterful, Grizel," he said, "and I dinna want to be, it was just for a minute that I liked the thought." She shook her head, but his next words had more effect. "If I had been that kind, would I have teached you Elspeth's prayer?"

"N-no, I don't think so," she said slowly, and perhaps he would have succeeded in soothing her, had not a sudden thought brought back the terror to her face.

"What is't now?" he asked.

"Oh, oh, oh!" she cried, "and I nearly went away with you!" and without another word she fled from the Den. She never told the doctor of this incident, and in time it became a mere shadow in the background, so that she was again his happy housekeeper, but that was because she had found strength to break with Tommy. She was only an eager little girl, pathetically ignorant about what she wanted most to understand, but she saw how an instinct had been fighting for her, and now it should not have to fight alone. How careful she became! All Tommy's wiles were vain, she would scarcely answer if he spoke to her; if he had ever possessed a power over her it was gone, Elspeth's prayer had saved her.

Jean Myles had told Tommy to teach that prayer to Elspeth; but who had told him to repeat it to Grizel?

CHAPTER XXXV

GRIZEL'S secession had at least one good effect: it gave Tommy more time in which to make a scholar of himself. Would you like a picture of Tommy trying to make a scholar of himself?

They all helped him in their different ways: Grizel, by declining his company; Corp, by being far away at Lookaboutyou, adding to the inches of a farm-house; Aaron Latta, by saying nothing, but looking "college or the herding;" Mr. McLean, who had settled down with Ailie at the Dovecot, by inquiries about his progress; Elspeth by — but did Elspeth's talks with him about how they should live in Aberdeen and afterward (when they were in the big house) do more than send his mind a-galloping (she holding on behind) along roads that lead not to Aberdeen? What drove Tommy oftenest to the weary drudgery was, perhaps, the alarm that came over him when he seemed of a sudden to hear the names of the bursars proclaimed and no Thomas Sandys among them. Then did he shudder, for well he knew that Aaron would

452

keep his threat, and he hastily covered the round table with books and sat for hours sorrowfully pecking at them, every little while to discover that his mind had soared to other things, when he hauled it back, as one draws in a reluctant kite. On these occasions Aaron seldom troubled him, except by glances that, nevertheless, brought the kite back more quickly than if they had been words of warning. If Elspeth was present the warper might sit moodily by the fire, but when the man and the boy were left together one or other of them soon retired, as if this was the only way of preserving the peace. Though determined to keep his word to Jean Myles liberally, Aaron had never liked Tommy, and Tommy's avoidance of him is easily accounted for; he knew that Aaron did not admire him, and unless you admired Tommy he was always a boor in your presence, shy and self-distrustful. Especially was this so if you were a lady (how amazingly he got on in after years with some of you, what agony others endured till he went away!), and it is the chief reason why there are such contradictory accounts of him to-day.

Sometimes Mr. Cathro had hopes of him other than those that could only be revealed in a shameful whisper with the door shut. "Not so bad," he might say to McLean; "if he keeps it up we may squeeze him through yet, without trusting to — to what I was fool enough to mention to you. The mathematics are his weak point, there's nothing practical about him (except when it's needed to carry out his devil's designs) and he cares not a doit about the line **A B**, nor what it's doing in the circle **K**, but there's whiles he surprises me when we're at Homer.   He has the spirit o't, man, even when he bogles at the sense."

But the next time Ivie called for a report—!

In his great days, so glittering, so brief (the days of the Penny Life) Tommy, looking back to this year was sure that he had never really tried to work.   But he had.   He did his very best, doggedly, wearily sitting at the round table till Elspeth feared that he was killing himself and gave him a melancholy comfort by saying so.   An hour afterward he might discover that he had been far away from his books, looking on at his affecting death and counting the mourners at the funeral.

Had he thought that Grizel's discovery was making her unhappy he would have melted at once, but never did she look so proud as when she scornfully passed him by, and he wagged his head complacently over her coming chagrin when she heard that he had carried the highest bursary. Then she would know what she had flung away. This should have helped him to another struggle with his lexicon, but it only provided a breeze for the kite, which flew so strong that he had to let go the string.

Aaron and the Dominie met one day in the square, and to Aaron's surprise Mr. Cathro's despondency about Tommy was more pronounced than before. " I wonder at that," the warper said, " for I assure you he has been harder at it than ever thae last nights. What's more, he used to look doleful as he sat at his table, but I notice now that he's as sweer to leave off as he's keen to begin, and the face of him is a' eagerness too, and he reads ower to himself what he has wrote and wags his head at it as if he thought it grand."

"Say you so?" asked Cathro, suspiciously; " does he leave what he writes lying about, Aaron?"

" No, but he takes it to you, does he no'?"

"Not him," said the Dominie, emphatically. " I may be mistaken, Aaron, but I'm doubting the young whelp is at his tricks again."

The Dominie was right, and before many days passed he discovered what was Tommy's new and delicious occupation.

For years Mr. Cathro had been in the habit of writing letters for such of the populace as could not guide a pen, and though he often told them not to come deaving him he liked the job, unexpected presents of a hen or a ham occasionally arriving as his reward, while the personal matters thus confided to him, as if he were a safe for the banking of private histories, gave him and his wife gossip for winter nights. Of late the number of his clients had decreased without his noticing it, so confident was he that they could not get on without him, but he received a shock at last from Andrew Dickie, who came one Saturday night with paper, envelope, a Queen's head, and a request for a letter for Bell Birse, now of Tilliedrum.

"You want me to speir in your name whether she'll have you, do you?" asked Cathro, with a flourish of his pen.

"It's no just so simple as that," said Andrew, and then he seemed to be rather at a loss to say what it was. "I dinna ken," he continued presently with a grave face, "whether you've noticed that I'm a gey queer deevil? Losh, I think I'm the queerest deevil I ken."

"We are all that," the Dominie assured him. "But what do you want me to write?"

"Well, it's like this," said Andrew; "I'm willing to marry her if she's agreeable, but I want to make sure that she'll take me afore I speir her. I'm a proud man, Dominie."

"You're a sly one!"

"Am I no!" said Andrew, well pleased. "Well, could you put the letter in that wy?"

"I wouldna," replied Mr. Cathro, "though I could, and I couldna though I would. It would defy the face of clay to do it, you canny lover."

Now, the Dominie had frequently declined to write as he was bidden, and had suggested altera-

456

tions which were invariably accepted, but to his astonishment Andrew would not give in. "I'll be stepping then," he said coolly, "for if you hinna the knack o't I ken somebody that has."

"Who?" demanded the irate Dominie.

"I promised no to tell you," replied Andrew, and away he went. Mr. Cathro expected him to return presently in humbler mood, but was disappointed, and a week or two afterwards he heard Andrew and Mary Jane Proctor cried in the parish church. "Did Bell Birse refuse him?" he asked the kirk officer, and was informed that Bell had never got a chance. "His letter was so cunning," said John, "that without speiring her, it drew ane frae her in which she let out that she was centered on Davit Allardyce."

"But who wrote Andrew's letter?" asked Mr. Cathro, sharply.

"I thought it had been yoursel'," said John, and the Dominie chafed, and lost much of the afternoon service by going over in his mind the names of possible rivals. He never thought of Tommy.

Then a week or two later fell a heavier blow. At least twice a year the Dominie had written for Meggy Duff to her daughter in Ireland a long letter founded on this suggestion, "Dear Kaytherine, if you dinna send ten shillings immediately, your puir auld mother will have neither house nor hame. I'm crying to you for't, Kaytherine; hearken and you'll hear my cry across the cauldriff sea." He met Meggy in the Banker's close one day, and asked her pleasantly if the time was not drawing nigh for another appeal. .

" I have wrote," replied the old woman, giving her pocket a boastful smack which she thus explained, "and it was the whole ten shillings this time, and you never got more for me than five."

" Who wrote the letter for you?" he asked, lowering.

She, too, it seemed, had promised not to tell.

"Did you promise to tell nobody, Meggy, or just no to tell me," he pressed her, of a sudden suspecting Tommy.

"Just no to tell you," she answered, and at that,

" Da-a-a," began the Dominie, and then saved his reputation by adding " gont." The derivation of the word dagont has puzzled many, but here we seem to have it.

It is interesting to know what Tommy wrote. The general opinion was that his letter must have been a triumph of eloquent appeal, and indeed he had first sketched out several masterpieces, all of some length and in different styles, but on the whole not unlike the concoctions of Meggy's former secretary; that is, he had dwelt on the duties of daughters, on the hardness of the times, on the certainty that if Katherine helped this time assistance would never be needed again. This sort of thing had always satisfied the Dominie, but Tommy, despite his several attempts, had a vague consciousness that there was something second-rate about them, and he tapped on his brain till it responded. The letter he despatched to Ireland, but had the wisdom not to read aloud even to Meggy, contained nothing save her own words, " Dear Kaytherine, if you dinna send ten shillings immediately your puir auld mother will have neither house nor hame. I'm crying to you for't, Kaytherine; hearken and you'll hear my cry across the cauldriff sea." It was a call from the heart which transported Katherine to Thrums in a second of time, she seemed to see her mother again, grown frail since last they met — and so all was well for Meggy. Tommy did not put all this to himself but he felt it, and after that he *could not* have written the letter differently. Happy Tommy! To be an artist is a great thing, but to be an artist and not know it is the most glorious plight in the world.

Other fickle clients put their correspondence into the boy's hands, and Cathro found it out but said nothing. Dignity kept him in check; he did not even let the tawse speak for him. So well did he dissemble that Tommy could not decide how much he knew, and dreaded his getting hold of some of the letters, yet pined to watch his face while he read them. This could not last forever. Mr. Cathro was like a haughty kettle which has choked its spout that none may know it has come a-boil, and we all know what in that event must happen sooner or later to the lid.

The three boys who had college in the tail of their eye had certain privileges not for the herd. It was taken for granted that when knowledge came their way they needed no overseer to make them stand their ground, and accordingly for great part of the day they had a back bench to themselves, with half-a-dozen hedges of boys and girls between them and the Dominie. From his chair Mr. Cathro could not see them, but a footboard was nailed to it, and when he stood on this, as he had an aggravating trick of doing, softly and swiftly, they were suddenly in view. A large fire had been burning all day, and the atmosphere was soporific. Mr. Cathro was so sleepy himself that the sight of a nodding head enraged him like a caricature, and he was on the footboard frequently for the reason that makes bearded men suck peppermints in church. Against his better judgment he took several peeps at Tommy, whom he had lately suspected of writing his letters in school, or at least of gloating over them on that back bench. To-day he was sure of it. However absorbing Euclid may be, even the forty-seventh of the first book does not make you chuckle and wag your head; you can bring a substantive in Virgil back to the verb that has lost it without looking as if you would like to exhibit them together in the square. But Tommy was thus elated until he gave way to grief of the most affecting kind. Now he looked gloomily before him as if all was over, now he buried his face in his hands, next his eyes were closed as if in prayer. All this the Dominie stood from him, but when at last he began to blubber —

At the blackboard was an arithmetic class, slates in hand, each member adding up aloud in turn a row of figures. By and by it was known that Cathro had ceased to listen. "Go on." his voice rather than himself said, and he accepted Mary Dundas's trembling assertion that four and seven make ten. Such was the faith in Cathro that even boys who could add promptly turned their eleven into ten, and he did not catch them at it. So obviously was his mind as well as his gaze on something beyond, that Sandy Riach, a wit who had been waiting his chance for years, snapped at it now, and roared " Ten and eleven, nineteen " (" Go on," said Cathro), "and four, twenty," gasped Sandy, " and eight, sixteen," he added, gaining courage. " Very good," murmured the Dominie, whereupon Sandy clenched his reputation forever by saying, in one glorious mouthful, "and six, eleven, and two, five, and one, nocht."

There was no laughing at it then (though Sandy

held a levee in the evening), they were all so stricken with amazement. By one movement they swung round to see what had fascinated Cathro, and the other classes doing likewise, Tommy became suddenly the centre of observation. Big tears were slinking down his face, and falling on some sheets of paper, which emotion prevented his concealing. Anon the unusual stillness in the school made him look up, but he was dazed, like one uncertain of his whereabouts, and he blinked rapidly to clear his eyes, as a bird shakes water from its wings.

Mr. Cathro first uttered what was afterward described as a kind of throttled skirl, and then he roared "Come here!" whereupon Tommy stepped forward heavily, and tried, as commanded, to come to his senses, but it was not easy to make so long a journey in a moment and several times, as he seemed about to conquer his tears, a wave of feeling set them flowing again.

"Take your time," said Mr. Cathro, grimly, "I can wait," and this had such a helpful effect that Tommy was able presently to speak up for his misdeeds. They consisted of some letters written at home, but brought to the school for private reading, and the Dominie got a nasty jar when he saw that they were all signed "Betsy Grieve." Miss Betsy Grieve, servant to Mr. Duthie, was about to marry, and these letters were acknow-

ledgments of wedding presents. Now, Mr. Cathro
had written similar letters for Betsy only a few
days before.

"Did she ask you to write these for her!" he
demanded, fuming, and Tommy replied demurely
that she had. He could not help adding, though
he felt the unwisdom of it, "She got some other
body to do them first, but his letters didna satisfy
her."

"Oh!" said Mr. Cathro, and it was such a vicious "oh" that Tommy squeaked tremblingly,
"I dinna know who he was."

Keeping his mouth shut by gripping his underlip with his teeth, the Dominie read the letters,
and Tommy gazed eagerly at him, all fear forgotten, soul conquering body. The others stood
or sat waiting, perplexed as to the cause, confident of the issue. The letters were much finer
productions than Cathro's, he had to admit it to
himself as he read. Yet the rivals had started fair,
for Betsy was a recent immigrant from Dunkeld
way, and the letters were to people known neither
to Tommy nor to the Dominie. Also, she had
given the same details for the guidance of each.
A lady had sent a teapot, which affected to be
new, but was not; Betsy recognised it by a scratch
on the lid, and wanted to scratch back, but politely. So Tommy wrote, "When you come to see
me we shall have a cup of tea out of your beauti-

ful present, and it will be like a meeting of three old friends." That was perhaps too polite, Betsy feared, but Tommy said authoritatively, "No, the politer the nippier."

There was a set of six cups and saucers from Peter something, who had loved Betsy in vain. She had shown the Dominie and Tommy the earrings given her long ago by Peter (they were bought with Sosh checks) and the poem he had written about them, and she was most anxious to gratify him in her reply. All Cathro could do, however, was to wish Peter well in some ornate sentences, while Tommy's was a letter that only a tender woman's heart could have indited, with such beautiful touches about the days which are no more, alas! forever, that Betsey listened to it with heaving breast and felt so sorry for her old swain that, forgetting she had never loved him, she all but gave Andrew the go-by and returned to Peter. As for Peter, who had been getting over his trouble, he saw now for the first time what he had lost, and he carried Betsy's dear letter in his oxter pocket and was inconsolable.

But the masterpiece went to Mrs. Dinnie, baker, in return for a flagon bun. Long ago her daughter, Janet, and Betsy had agreed to marry on the same day, and many a quip had Mrs. Dinnie cast at their romantic compact. But Janet died, and so it was a sad letter that Tommy had to write to her mother. "I'm doubting you're no auld enough for this ane," soft-hearted Betsy said, but she did not know her man. "Tell me some one thing the mother used often to say when she was taking her fun off the pair of you," he said, and "Where is she buried?" was a suggestive question, with the happy tag, "Is there a tree hanging over the grave?" Thus assisted, he composed a letter that had a tear in every sentence. Betsy rubbed her eyes red over it, and not all its sentiments were allowed to die, for Mrs. Dinnie, touched to to the heart, printed the best of them in black licorice on short bread for funeral feasts, at which they gave rise to solemn reflections as they went down.

Nevertheless, this letter affected none so much as the writer of it. His first rough sketch became so damp as he wrote that he had to abandon his pen and take to pencil; while he was revising he had often to desist to dry his eyes on the coverlet of Aaron's bed, which made Elspeth weep also, though she had no notion what he was at. But when the work was finished he took her into the secret and read his letter to her, and he almost choked as he did so. Yet he smiled rapturously through his woe, and she knew no better than to be proud of him, and he awoke next morning with a cold, brought on you can see how, but his triumph was worth its price.

Having read the letter in an uncanny silence, Mr. Cathro unbottled Tommy for the details, and out they came with a rush, blowing away the cork discretion. Yet was the Dominie slow to strike; he seemed to find more satisfaction in surveying his young friend with a wondering gaze that had a dash of admiration in it, which Tommy was the first to note.

"I don't mind admitting before the whole school," said Mr. Cathro, slowly, "that if these letters had been addressed to me they would have taken me in."

Tommy tried to look modest, but his chest would have its way.

"You little sacket," cried the Dominie, "how did you manage it?"

"I think I thought I was Betsy at the time," Tommy answered, with proper awe.

"She told me nothing about the weeping-willow at the grave," said the Dominie, perhaps in self-defence.

"You hadna speired if there was one," retorted Tommy, jealously.

"What made you think of it?"

"I saw it might come in neat." (He had said in the letter that the weeping-willow reminded him of the days when Janet's bonny hair hung down kissing her waist 'ust as the willow kissed the grave.)

"Willows don't hang so low as you seem to think," said the Dominie.

"Yes, they do," replied Tommy; "I walked three miles to see one to make sure. I was near putting in another beautiful bit about weeping-willows."

"Well, why didn't you?"

Tommy looked up with an impudent snigger. "You could never guess," he said.

"Answer me at once," thundered his preceptor.

"Was it because ——"

"No," interrupted Tommy, so conscious of Mr. Cathro's inferiority that to let him go on seemed waste of time. "It was because, though it is a beautiful thing in itself, I felt a servant lassie wouldna have thought o't. I was sweer," he admitted, with a sigh; then firmly, "but I cut it out."

Again Cathro admired, reluctantly. The hack does feel the difference between himself and the artist. Cathro might possibly have had the idea, he could not have cut it out.

But the hack is sometimes, or usually, or nearly always the artist's master, and can make him suffer for his dem'd superiority.

"What made you snivel when you read the pathetic bits?" asked Cathro, with itching fingers.

"I was so sorry for Peter and Mrs. Dinnie," Tommy answered, a little puzzled himself now. "I saw them so clear."

"And yet until Betsy came to you, you had never heard tell of them?"

"No."

"And on reflection you don't care a doit about them?"

"N-no."

"And you care as little for Betsy?"

"No now, but at the time I a kind of thought I was to be married to Andrew."

"And even while you blubbered you were saying to yourself, 'What a clever billie I am!'"

Mr. Cathro had certainly intended to end the scene with the strap, but as he stretched out his hand for it he had another idea. "Do you know why Nether Drumgley's sheep are branded with the letters N. D.?" he asked his pupils, and a dozen replied, "So as all may ken wha they belong to."

"Precisely," said Mr. Cathro, "and similarly they used to brand a letter on a felon, so that all might know whom *he* belonged to." He crossed to the fireplace, and, picking up a charred stick, wrote with it on the forehead of startled Tommy the letters "S. T."

"Now," said the Dominie complacently, "we know to whom Tommy belongs."

All were so taken aback that for some seconds nothing could be heard save Tommy indignantly wiping his brow; then " Wha is he?" cried one, the mouthpiece of half a hundred.

" He is one of the two proprietors we have just been speaking of," replied Cathro, dryly, and turning again to Tommy, he said, " Wipe away, Sentimental Tommy, try hot water, try cold water, try a knife, but you will never get those letters off you; you are branded for ever and ever."

CHAPTER XXXVI

OF FOUR MINISTERS WHO AFTERWARDS BOASTED THAT THEY HAD KNOWN TOMMY SANDYS

BURSARY examination time had come, and to the siege of Aberdeen marched a hungry half-dozen—three of them from Thrums, two from the Glenquharity school. The sixth was Tod Lindertis, a ploughman from the Dubb of Prosen, his place of study the bothy after lousing time (Do you hear the klink of quoits?) or a one-roomed house near it, his tutor a dogged little woman, who knew not the accusative from the dative, but never tired of holding the book while Tod recited. Him someone greets with the good-natured jeer, "It's your fourth try, is it no, Tod?" and he answers cheerily, "It is, my lathie, and I'll keep kick, kick, kicking away to the nth time."

"Which means till the door flies open," says the dogged little woman, who is the gallant Tod's no less gallant wife, and already the mother of two. I hope Tod will succeed this time.

The competitors, who were to travel part of the way on their shanks, met soon after daybreak in Cathro's yard, where a little crowd awaited them,

parents trying to look humble, Mr. Duthie and
Ramsay Cameron thinking of the morning when
they set off on the same errand — but the results
were different, and Mr. Duthie is now a minister,
and Ramsay is in the middle of another wob. Both
dominies were present, hating each other for that
day only, up to the mouth, where their icy polite-
ness was a thing to shudder at, and each was
drilling his detachment to the last moment, but
by different methods; for while Mr. Cathro entreated Joe Meldrum for God's sake to mind that
about the genitive, and Willie Simpson to keep
his mouth shut and drink even water sparingly,
Mr. Ogilvy cracked jokes with Gav Dishart and
explained them to Lauchlan McLauchlan. "Think
of anything now but what is before you," was Mr.
Ogilvy's advice. "Think of nothing else," roared
Mr. Cathro. But though Mr. Ogilvy seemed
outwardly calm it was base pretence; his dickie
gradually wriggled through the opening of his
waistcoat, as if bearing a protest from his inward
parts, and he let it hang crumpled and conspicu-
ous, while Grizel, on the outskirts of the crowd,
yearned to put it right.

Grizel was not there; she told several people,
including herself, to say good-by to Tommy, and
oh, how she scorned Elspeth for looking as if life
would not be endurable without him. Knowing
what Elspeth was, Tommy had decided that she

should not accompany him to the yard (of course she was to follow him to Aberdeen if he distinguished himself — Mr. McLean had promised to bring her), but she told him of her dream that he headed the bursary list, and as this dream coincided with some dreams of his own, though not with all, it seemed to give her such fortitude that he let her come. An expressionless face was Tommy's, so that not even the experienced dominie of Glenquharity, covertly scanning his rival's lot, could tell whether he was gloomy or uplifted; he did not seem to be in need of a long sleep like Willie Simpson, nor were his eyes glazed like Gav Dishart's, who carried all the problems of Euclid before him on an invisible blackboard and dared not even wink lest he displaced them, nor did he, like Tod Lindertis, answer questions about his money pocket or where he had stowed his bread and cheese with

"After envy, spare, obey,
The dative put, remember, pray."

Mr. Ogilvy noticed that Cathro tapped his forehead, doubtfully, every time his eyes fell on Tommy, but otherwise shunned him, and he asked, "What are his chances?"

"That's the laddie," replied Mr. Cathro, "who, when you took her ladyship to see Corp Shiach years ago impersona —— "

"I know," Mr. Ogilvy interrupted him hastily, "but how will he stand, think you?"

Mr. Cathro coughed. "We'll see," he said guardedly.

Nevertheless Tommy was not to get round the corner without betraying a little of himself, for Elspeth, having borne up magnificently when he shook hands, screamed at the tragedy of his back and fell into the arms of Tod's wife, whereupon Tommy first tried to brazen it out and then kissed her in the presence of a score of witnesses, including Grizel, who stamped her foot, though what right had she to be so angry? "I'm sure," Elspeth sobbed, "that the professor would let me sit beside you; I would just hunker on the floor and hold your foot and no say a word." Tommy gave Todd's wife an imploring look, and she managed to comfort Elspeth with predictions of his coming triumph and the reunion to follow. Grateful Elspeth in return asked Tommy to help Tod when the professors were not looking, and he promised, after which she had no more fear for Tod.

And now, ye drums that we all carry in our breasts, beat your best over the bravest sight ever seen in a small Scotch town of an autumn morning, the departure of its fighting lads for the lists at Aberdeen. Let the tune be the sweet familiar one you found somewhere in the Bible long ago, "The mothers we leave behind us"—leave behind us on their knees. May it dirl through your bones, brave boys, to the end, as you hope not to be damned. And now, quick march.

A week has elapsed, and now — there is no call for music now, for these are but the vanquished crawling back, Joe Meldrum and — and another. No, it is not Tod, he stays on in Aberdeen, for he is a twelve-pound tenner. The two were within a mile of Thrums at three o'clock, but after that they lagged, waiting for the gloaming, when they stole to their homes, ducking as they passed windows without the blinds down. Elspeth ran to Tommy when he appeared in the doorway, and then she got quickly between him and Aaron. The warper was sitting by the fire at his evening meal, and he gave the wanderer a long steady look, then without a word returned to his porridge and porter. It was a less hearty welcome home even than Joe's; his mother was among those who had wept to lose her son, but when he came back to her she gave him a whack on the head with the thieval.

Aaron asked not a question about those days in Aberdeen, but he heard a little about them from Elspeth. Tommy had not excused himself to Elspeth, he had let her do as she liked with his head (this was a great treat to her), and while it lay pressed against hers, she made remarks about Aberdeen professors which it would have done them good to hear. These she repeated to Aaron, who was about to answer roughly, and then suddenly put her on his knee instead.

"They didna ask the right questions," she told him, and when the warper asked if Tommy had said so, she declared that he had refused to say a word against them, which seemed to her to cover him with glory. "But he doubted they would make that mistake afore he started," she said brightly, "so you see he saw through them afore he ever set eyes on them."

Corp would have replied admiringly to this "Oh, the little deevil!" When he heard of Tommy's failure he wanted to fight Gav Dishart and Willie Simpson, but Aaron was another kind of confidant, and even when she explained on Tommy's authority that there are two kinds of cleverness, the kind you learn from books and a kind that is inside yourself, which latter was Tommy's kind, he only replied:

"He can take it wi' him to the herding, then, and see if it'll keep the cattle frae stravaiging."

"It's no that kind of cleverness either," said Elspeth, quaking, and quaked also Tommy, who had gone to the garret, to listen through the floor.

"No? I would like to ken what use his cleverness can be put to, then," said Aaron, and Elspeth answered nothing, and Tommy only sighed, for that indeed was the problem. But though to these

475

three and to Cathro, and to Mr. and Mrs. McLean and to others more mildly interested, it seemed a problem beyond solution, there was one in Thrums who rocked her arms at their denseness, a girl growing so long in the legs that twice within the last year she had found it necessary to let down her parramatty frock. As soon as she heard that Tommy had come home vanquished, she put on the quaint blue bonnet with the white strings, in which she fondly believed she looked ever so old (her period of mourning was at an end, but she still wore her black dress), and forgetting all except that he was unhappy, she ran to a certain little house to comfort him. But she did not go in, for through the window she saw Elspeth petting him, and that somehow annoyed her. In the evening, however, she called on Mr. Cathro.

Perhaps you want to know why she, who at last saw Sentimental Tommy in his true light and spurned him accordingly, now exerted herself in his behalf instead of going on with the papering of the surgery. Well, that was the reason. She had put the question to herself before — not, indeed, before going to Monypenny, but before calling on the Dominie — and decided that she wanted to send Tommy to college, because she disliked him so much that she could not endure the prospect of his remaining in Thrums. Now, are you satisfied?

She could scarcely take time to say good-evening to Mr. Cathro before telling him the object of her visit. "The letters Tommy has been writing for people are very clever, are they not?" she began.

"You've heard of them, have you?"

"Everybody has heard of them," she said injudiciously, and he groaned and asked if she had come to tell him this. But he admitted their cleverness, whereupon she asked, "Well, if he is clever at writing letters, would he not be clever at writing an essay?"

"I wager my head against a snuff mull that he would be, but what are you driving at?"

"I was wondering whether he could not win the prize I heard Dr. McQueen speaking about, the — is it not called the Hugh Blackadder?"

"My head against a buckie that he could! Sit down, Grizel, I see what you mean now. Ay, but the pity is he's not eligible for the Hugh Blackadder. Oh, that he was, oh, that he was! I would make Ogilvy of Glenquharity sing small at last! His loons have carried the Blackadder for the last seven years without a break. The Hugh Blackadder Mortification, the bequest is called, and, 'deed, it has been a sore mortification to me!"

Calming down, he told her the story of the bequest. Hugh Blackadder was a Thrums man who made a fortune in America, and bequeathed the interest of three hundred pounds of it to be competed for yearly by the youth of his native place. He had grown fond of Thrums and all its ways over there, and left directions that the prize should be given for the best essay in the Scots tongue, the ministers of the town and glens to be the judges, the competitors to be boys who were going to college but had not without it the wherewithal to support themselves. The ministers took this to mean that those who carried small bursaries were eligible, and indeed it had usually gone to a bursar.

"Sentimental Tommy would not have been able to compete if he had got a bursary," Mr. Cathro explained, "because however small it was Mr. McLean meant to double it; and he can't compete without it, for McLean refuses to help him now (he was here an hour since, saying the laddie was obviously hopeless), so I never thought of entering Tommy for the Blackadder. No, it will go to Ogilvy's Lauchlan McLauchlan, who is a twelve-pounder, and, as there can be no competitors he'll get it without the trouble of coming back to write the essay."

"But suppose Mr. McLean were willing to do what he promised if Tommy won the Blackadder?"

"It's useless to appeal to McLean. He's hard

set against the laddie now and washes his hands of him, saying that Aaron Latta is right after all. He may soften, and get Tommy into a trade to save him from the herding, but send him to college he won't, and indeed he's right, the laddie's a fool."

"Not at writing let ——"

"And what is the effect of his letter-writing, but to make me ridiculous? Me! I wonder you can expect me to move a finger for him; he has been my torment ever since his inscrutable face appeared at my door."

"Never mind him," said Grizel, cunningly. "But think what a triumph it would be to you if your boy beat Mr. Ogilvy's."

The dominie rose in his excitement and slammed the table. " My certie, lassie, but it would!" he cried. "Ogilvy looks on the Black-adder as his perquisite, and he's surer of it than ever this year. And there's no doubt but Tommy would carry it. My head to a buckie preen he would carry it, and then, oh, for a sight of Ogil-vy's face, oh, for —— " He broke off abruptly. "But what's the good of thinking of it?" he said, dolefully. "Mr. McLean's a firm man when he makes up his mind."

Nevertheless, though McLean, who had a Scotch-man's faith in the verdict of professors, and had been bitterly disappointed by Tommy's failure, refused to be converted by the Dominie's entreaties, he yielded to them when they were voiced by Ailie (brought into the plot *vice* Grizel retired), and Elspeth got round Aaron, and so it came about that with his usual luck, Tommy was given another chance, present at the competition, which took place in the Thrums school, the Rev. Mr. Duthie, the Rev. Mr. Dishart, the Rev. Mr. Gloag of Noran Side, the Rev. Mr. Lorrimer of Glenquharity (these on hair-bottomed chairs), and Mr. Cathro and Mr. Ogilvy (cane); present also to a less extent (that is to say, their faces at the windows), Corp and others who applauded the local champion when he entered and derided McLauchlan. The subject of the essay was changed yearly, this time "A Day in Church" was announced, and immediately Lauchlan McLauchlan, who had not missed a service since his scarlet fever year (and too few then), smote his red head in agony, while Tommy, who had missed as many as possible, looked calmly confident. For two hours the competitors were put into a small room communicating with the larger one, and Tommy began at once with a confident smirk that presently gave way to a most holy expression; while Lauchlan gaped at him and at last got started also, but had to pause occasionally to rub his face on his sleeve, for, like Corp, he was one of the kind who cannot think without perspiring. In the large room the ministers gossiped about eternal punishment, and of the two dominies one sat at his ease, like a passenger who knows that the coach will reach the goal without any exertion on his part, while the other paced the floor, with many a despondent glance through the open door whence the scraping proceeded; and the one was pleasantly cool; and the other in a plot of heat; and the one made genial remarks about everyday matters, and the answers of the other stood on their heads. It was a familiar comedy to Mr. Ogilvy, hardly a variation on what had happened five times in six for many years: the same scene, the same scraping in the little room, the same background of ministers (blackaviced Mr. Lorrimer had begun to bark again), the same dominies; everything was as it had so often been, except that he and Cathro had changed places; it was Cathro who sat smiling now and Mr. Ogilvy who dolefully paced the floor.

To be able to write! Throughout Mr. Ogilvy's life, save when he was about one and twenty, this had seemed the great thing, and he ever approached the thought reverently, as if it were a maid of more than mortal purity. And it is, and because he knew this she let him see her face, which shall ever be hidden from those who look not for the soul, and to help him nearer to her came assistance in strange guise, the loss of loved ones, dolour unutterable; but still she was beyond his reach.

Night by night, when the only light in the glen was the schoolhouse lamp, of use at least as a landmark to solitary travellers—who miss it nowadays, for it burns no more—she hovered over him, nor did she deride his hopeless efforts, but rather as she saw him go from black to gray and from gray to white in her service, were her luminous eyes sorrowful because she was not for him, and she bent impulsively toward him, so that once or twice in a long life he touched her fingers, and a heavenly spark was lit, for he had risen higher than himself, and that is literature.

He knew that oblivion was at hand, ready to sweep away his pages almost as soon as they were filled (Do we not all hear her besom when we pause to dip?), but he had done his best and he had a sense of humour, and perhaps some day would come a pupil of whom he could make what he had failed to make of himself. That prodigy never did come, though it was not for want of nursing, and there came at last, in succession most maddening to Mr. Cathro, a row of youths who could be trained to carry the Hugh Blackadder. Mr. Ogilvy's many triumphs in this competition had not dulled his appetite for more, and depressed he was at the prospect of a reverse. That it was coming now he could not doubt. McLauchlan, who was to be Rev., had a flow of words (which would prevent his perspiring much in the pulpit),

but he could no more describe a familiar scene
with the pen than a milkmaid can draw a cow.
The Thrums representatives were sometimes as
little gifted, it is true, and never were they so well
exercised, but this Tommy had the knack of it,
as Mr. Ogilvy could not doubt, for the story of his
letter-writing had been through the glens.

"Keep up your spirits," Mr. Lorrimer had
said to him as they walked together to the fray,
"Cathro's loon may compose the better of the
two, but, as I understand, the first years of his life
were spent in London, and so he may bogle at the
Scotch."

But the Dominie replied, " Don't buoy me up
on a soap bubble. If there's as much in him as I
fear, that should be a help to him instead of a
hindrance, for it will have set him a-thinking about
the words he uses."

And the satisfaction on Tommy's face when the
subject of the essay was given out, with the busi-
ness-like way in which he set to work, had added
to the Dominie's misgivings; if anything was re-
quired to dishearten him utterly it was provided
by Cathro's confident smile. The two Thrums
ministers were naturally desirous that Tommy
should win, but the younger of them was very
fond of Mr. Ogilvy, and noticing his unhappy
peeps through the door dividing the rooms, proposed that it should be closed. He shut it him-

self, and as he did so he observed that Tommy was biting his pen and frowning, while McLauchlan, having ceased to think, was getting on nicely. But it did not strike Mr. Dishart that this was worth commenting on.

"Are you not satisfied with the honours you have already got, you greedy man?" he said, laying his hand affectionately on Mr. Ogilvy, who only sighed for reply.

"It is well that the prize should go to different localities, for in that way its sphere of usefulness is extended," remarked pompous Mr. Gloag, who could be impartial, as there was no candidate from Noran Side. He was a minister much in request for church soirees, where he amused the congregations so greatly with personal anecdote about himself that they never thought much of him afterwards. There is one such minister in every presbytery.

"And to have carried the Hugh Blackadder seven times running is surely enough for any one locality, even though it be Glenquharity," said Mr. Lorrimer, preparing for defeat.

"There's consolation for you, sir," said Mr. Cathro, sarcastically, to his rival, who tried to take snuff in sheer bravado, but let it slip through his fingers, and after that until the two hours were up, the talk was chiefly of how Tommy would get on at Aberdeen. But it was confined to the four ministers and one dominie. Mr. Ogilvy still hovered about the door of communication, and his face fell more and more, making Mr. Dishart quite unhappy.

"I'm an old fool," the Dominie admitted, "but I can't help being cast down. The fact is that — I have only heard the scrape of one pen for nearly an hour."

"Poor Lauchlan!" exclaimed Mr. Cathro, rubbing his hands gleefully, and indeed it was such a shameless exhibition that the Auld Licht minister said reproachfully, "You forget yourself, Mr. Cathro, let us not be unseemly exalted in the hour of our triumph."

Then Mr. Cathro sat upon his hands as the best way of keeping them apart, but the moment Mr. Dishart's back presented itself, he winked at Mr. Ogilvy.

He winked a good deal more presently.

For after all—how to tell it! Tommy was ignominiously beaten, making such a beggarly show that the judges thought it unnecessary to take the essays home with them for leisurely consideration before pronouncing Mr. Lauchlan Mc-Lauchlan winner. There was quite a commotion in the school-room. At the end of the allotted time the two competitors had been told to hand in their essays, and how Mr. McLauchlan was sniggering is not worth recording, so dumfounded,

confused and raging was Tommy. He clung to
his papers, crying fiercely that the two hours could
not be up yet, and Lauchlan having tried to keep
the laugh in too long it exploded in his mouth,
whereupon, said he, with a guffaw, "He hasna
written a word for near an hour!"

"What! It was you I heard!" cried Mr.
Ogilvy, gleaming, while the unhappy Cathro tore
the essay from Tommy's hands. Essay! It was
no more an essay than a twig is a tree, for the
gowk had stuck in the middle of his second page.
Yes, stuck is the right expression, as his chagrined
teacher had to admit when the boy was cross-ex-
amined. He had not been "up to some of his
tricks," he had stuck, and his explanations, as you
will admit, merely emphasized his incapacity.

He had brought himself to public scorn for lack
of a word. What word? they asked testily, but
even now he could not tell. He had wanted a
Scotch word that would signify how many people
were in church, and it was on the tip of his tongue
but would come no farther. Puckle was nearly
the word, but it did not mean so many people as
he meant. The hour had gone by just like winking; he had forgotten all about time while searching his mind for the word.

When Mr. Ogilvy heard this he seemed to be
much impressed, repeatedly he nodded his head
as some beat time to music, and he muttered

to himself, "The right word — yes, that's everything," and "'the time went by like winking' —
exactly, precisely," and he would have liked to
examine Tommy's bumps, but did not, nor said
a word aloud, for was he not there in McLauchlan's interest?

The other five were furious; even Mr. Lorrimer,
though his man had won, could not smile in face
of such imbecility. "You little tattie-doolie,"
Cathro roared, "were there not a dozen words to
wile from if you had an ill-will to puckle? What
ailed you at manzy, or ——"

"I thought of manzy," replied Tommy woefully, for he was ashamed of himself, "but — but
a manzy's a swarm. It would mean that the folk
in the kirk were buzzing thegither like bees, instead of sitting still."

"Even if it does mean that," said Mr. Duthie,
with impatience, "what was the need of being so
particular? Surely the art of essay-writing con-
sists in using the first word that comes and hurrying on."

"That's how I did," said the proud McLauchlan, who is now leader of a party in the church,
and a figure in Edinburgh during the month of
May.

"I see," interposed Mr. Gloag, "that McLauchlan speaks of there being a mask of people in the
church. Mask is a fine Scotch word."

" Admirable," assented Mr. Dishart.

" I thought of mask," whimpered Tommy, " but that would mean the kirk was crammed, and I just meant it to be middling full."

" Flow would have done," suggested Mr. Lorimer.

" Flow's but a handful," said Tommy.

" Curran, then, you jackanapes ! "

" Curran's no enough."

Mr. Lorrimer flung up his hands in despair.

" I wanted something between curran and mask," said Tommy, dogged, yet almost at the crying.

Mr. Ogilvy, who had been hiding his admiration with difficulty, spread a net for him. " You said you wanted a word that meant middling full. Well, why did you not say middling full — or fell mask ? "

" Yes, why not ? " demanded the ministers, unconsciously caught in the net.

" I wanted one word," replied Tommy, unconsciously avoiding it.

" You jewel ! " muttered Mr. Ogilvy under his breath, but Mr. Cathro would have banged the boy's head had not the ministers interfered.

" It is so easy, too, to find the right word," said Mr. Gloag.

" It's no ; it's as difficult as to hit a squirrel," cried Tommy, and again Mr. Ogilvy nodded approval.

But the ministers were only pained.

"The lad is merely a numskull," said Mr. Dishart, kindly.

"And no teacher could have turned him into anything else," said Mr. Duthie.

"And so, Cathro, you need not feel sore over your defeat," added Mr. Gloag; but nevertheless Cathro took Tommy by the neck and ran him out of the parish school of Thrums. When he returned to the others he found the ministers congratulating McLauchlan, whose nose was in the air, and complimenting Mr. Ogilvy, who listened to their formal phrases solemnly and accepted their hand-shakes with a dry chuckle.

"Ay, grin away, sir," the mortified dominie of Thrums said to him sourly, "the joke is on your side."

"You are right, sir," replied Mr. Ogilvy, mysteriously, "the joke is on my side, and the best of it is that not one of you knows what the joke is!"

And then an odd thing happened. As they were preparing to leave the school, the door opened a little and there appeared in the aperture the face of Tommy, tear-stained but excited. "I ken the word now," he cried, "it came to me a' at once; it is hantle!"

The door closed with a victorious bang, just in time to prevent Cathro ——

"Oh, the sumph!" exclaimed Mr. Lauchlan

McLauchlan, "as if it mattered what the word is now!"

And said Mr. Dishart, "Cathro, you had better tell Aaron Latta that the sooner he sends this nincompoop to the herding the better."

But Mr. Ogilvy giving his Lauchlan a push that nearly sent him sprawling, said in an ecstasy to himself, "He *had* to think of it till he got it — and he got it. The laddie is a genius!" They were about to tear up Tommy's essay, but he snatched it from them and put it in his outer pocket. "I am a collector of curiosities," he explained, "and this paper may be worth money yet."

"Well," said Cathro, savagely, "I have one satisfaction, I ran him out of my school."

"Who knows," replied Mr. Ogilvy, "but what you may be proud to dust a chair for him when he comes back?"

CHAPTER XXXVII

THE END OF A BOYHOOD

CONVINCED of his own worthlessness, Tommy was sufficiently humble now, but Aaron Latta, nevertheless, marched to the square on the following market day and came back with the boy's sentence, Elspeth being happily absent.

" I say nothing about the disgrace you have brought on this house," the warper began without emotion, " for it has been a shamed house since afore you were born, and it's a small offence to skail on a clarty floor. But now I've done more for you than I promised Jean Myles to do, and you had your pick atween college and the herding, and the herding you've chosen twice. I call you no names, you ken best what you're fitted for, but I've seen the farmer of the Dubb of Prosen the day, and he was short-handed through the loss of Tod Lindertis, so you're fee'd to him. Dinna think you get Tod's place, it'll be years afore you rise to that, but it's right and proper that as he steps up, you should step down."

" The Dubb of Prosen ! " cried Tommy in dis-
may. " It's fifteen miles frae here."

" It's a' that."

" But — but — but Elspeth and me never thought
of my being so far away that she couldna see me.
We thought of a farmer near Thrums."

" The farther you're frae her the better," said
Aaron, uneasily, yet honestly believing what he
said.

" It'll kill her," Tommy cried fiercely. With
only his own suffering to consider he would probably have nursed it into a play through which he
stalked as the noble child of misfortune, but in his
anxiety for Elspeth he could still forget himself.
" Fine you ken she canna do without me," he
screamed.

" She maun be weaned," replied the warper,
with a show of temper; he was convinced that
the sooner Elspeth learned to do without Tommy
the better it would be for herself in the end, but
in his way of regarding the boy there was also a
touch of jealousy, pathetic rather than forbidding.
To him he left the task of breaking the news to
Elspeth; and Tommy, terrified lest she should
swoon under it, was almost offended when she remained calm. But, alas, the reason was that she
thought she was going with him.

· " Will we have to walk all the way to the Dubb
of Prosen ? " she asked, quite brightly, and at that

Tommy twisted about in misery. " You are no
— you canna — " he began, and then dodged the
telling. " We — we may get a lift in a cart," he
said weakly.

" And I'll sit aside you in the fields, and make
chains o' the gowans, will I no ? Speak, Tommy!"

" Ay — ay, will you," he groaned.

" And we'll have a wee, wee room to oursel's,
and —— "

He broke down. " Oh, Elspeth," he cried, " it
was ill-done of me no to stick to my books, and
get a bursary, and it was waur o' me to bother
about that word. I'm a scoundrel, I am, I'm a
black, I'm a —— "

But she put her hand on his mouth, saying,
" I'm fonder o' you than ever, Tommy, and I'll
like the Dubb o' Prosen fine, and what does it
matter where we are when we're thegither?"
which was poor comfort for him, but still he could
not tell her the truth, and so in the end Aaron had
to tell her. It struck her down, and the doctor
had to be called in during the night to stop her
hysterics. When at last she fell asleep Tommy's
arm was beneath her, and by and by it was in
agony, but he set his teeth and kept it there rather
than risk waking her.

When Tommy was out of the way, Aaron did
his clumsy best to soothe her, sometimes half-
shamefacedly pressing her cheek to his, and she

did not repel him, but there was no response. " Dinna take on in that way, dawtie," he would say, " I'll be good to you."

" But you're no Tommy," Elspeth answered.

" I'm not, I'm but a stunted tree, blasted in my youth, but for a' that, I would like to have somebody to care for me, and there's none to do't, Elspeth, if you winna. I'll gang walks wi' you. I'll take you to the fishing, I'll come to the garret at night to hap you up, I'll — I'll teach you the games I used to play mysel'. I'm no sure but what you might make something o' me yet, bairn, if you tried hard."

" But you're no Tommy," Elspeth wailed again, and when he advised her to put Tommy out of her mind for a little and speak of other things, she only answered innocently, " What else is there to speak about ? "

Mr. McLean had sent Tommy a pound, and so was done with him, but Ailie still thought him a dear, though no longer a wonder, and Elspeth took a strange confession to her, how one night she was so angry with God that she had gone to bed without saying her prayers. She had just meant to keep Him in suspense for a little, and then say them, but she fell asleep. And that was not the worst, for when she woke in the morning, and saw that she was still living, she was glad she had not said them. But next night she said them twice.

And this, too, is another flash into her dark character. Tommy, who never missed saying his prayers and could say them with surprising quickness, told her, " God is fonder of lonely lasses than of any other kind, and every time you greet it makes Him greet, and when you're cheerful it makes Him cheerful too." This was meant to dry her eyes, but it had not that effect, for, said Elspeth, vindictively, " Well, then, I'll just make Him as miserable as I can."

When Tommy was merely concerned with his own affairs he did not think much about God, but he knew that no other could console Elspeth, and his love for her usually told him the right things to say, and while he said them he was quite carried away by his sentiments and even wept over them, but within the hour he might be leering. They were beautiful, and were repeated of course to Mrs. McLean, who told her husband of them, declaring that this boy's love for his sister made her a better woman.

" But nevertheless," said Ivie, " Mr. Cathro assures me —— "

" He is prejudiced," retorted Mrs. McLean warmly, prejudice being a failing which all women marvel at. " Just listen to what the boy said to Elspeth to-day. He said to her, ' When I am away, try for a whole day to be better than you ever were before, and think of nothing else, and then when prayer-time comes you will see that you have been happy without knowing it.' Fancy his finding that out."

"I wonder if he ever tried it himself?" said Mr. McLean.

"Ivie, think shame of yourself!"

"Well, even Cathro admits that he has a kind of cleverness, but ——"

"Cleverness!" exclaimed Ailie, indignantly, "that is not cleverness, it is holiness;" and leaving the cynic she sought Elspeth, and did her good by pointing out that a girl who had such a brother should try to save him pain. "He is very miserable, dear," she said, "because you are so unhappy. If you looked brighter, think how that would help him, and it would show that you are worthy of him." So Elspeth went home trying hard to look brighter, but made a sad mess of it.

"Think of getting letters frae me every time the post comes in!" said Tommy, and then indeed her face shone.

And then Elspeth could write to him—yes, as often as ever she liked! This pleased her even more. It was such an exquisite thought that she could not wait, but wrote the first one before he started, and he answered it across the table. And Mrs. McLean made a letter-bag, with two strings to it, and showed her how to carry it about with her in a safer place than a pocket.

496

Then a cheering thing occurred. Came Corp. with the astounding news that, in the Glenquharity dominie's opinion, Tommy should have got the Hugh Blackadder.

"He says he is glad he wasna judge, because he would have had to give you the prize, and he laughs like to split at the ministers for giving it to Lauchlan McLauchlan."

Now, great was the repute of Mr. Ogilvy, and Tommy gaped incredulous. "He had no word of that at the time," he said.

"No likely! He says if the ministers was so doited as to think his loon did best, it wasna for him to conter them."

"Man, Corp, you ca' me aff my feet! How do you ken this?"

Corp had promised not to tell, and he thought he did not tell, but Tommy was too clever for him. Grizel, it appeared, had heard Mr. Ogilvy saying this strange thing to the doctor, and she burned to pass it on to Tommy, but she could not carry it to him herself, because — Why was it? Oh, yes, because she hated him. So she made a messenger of Corp, and warned him against telling who had sent him with the news.

Half enlightened, Tommy began to strut again. "You see there's something in me for all they say," he told Elspeth. "Listen to this. At the bursary examinations there was some English we had to turn into Latin, and it said, 'No man ever attained supreme eminence who worked for mere lucre; such efforts must ever be bounded by base mediocrity. None shall climb high but he who climbs for love, for in truth where the heart is, there alone shall the treasure be found.' Elspeth, it came ower me in a clink how true that was, and I sat saying it to myself, though I saw Gav Dishart and Willie Simpson and the rest beginning to put it into Latin at once, as little ta'en up wi' the words as if they had been about auld Hannibal. I aye kent, Elspeth, that I could never do much at the learning, but I didna see the reason till I read that. Syne I kent that playing so real-like in the Den, and telling about my fits when it wasna me that had them but Corp, and mourning for Lewis Doig's father, and writing letters for folk so grandly, and a' my other queer ploys that ended in Cathro's calling me Sentimental Tommy, was what my heart was in, and I saw in a jiffy that if thae things were work, I should soon rise to supreme eminence."

"But they're no," said Elspeth, sadly.

"No," he admitted, his face falling, "but, Elspeth, if I was to hear some day of work I could put my heart into as if it were a game! I wouldna be lang in finding the treasure syne. Oh, the blatter I would make!"

"I doubt there's no sic work," she answered,

but he told her not to be so sure. "I thought
there wasna mysel'," he said, "till now, but sure
as death my heart was as ta'en up wi' hunting for
the right word as if it had been a game, and that
was how the time slipped by so quick. Yet it
was paying work, for the way I did it made Mr.
Ogilvy see I should have got the prize, and a'
body kens there's more cleverness in him than in
a cart-load o' ministers."

"But, but there are no more Hugh Blackadders
to try for, Tommy?"

"That's nothing, there maun be other work o'
the same kind. Elspeth, cheer up, I tell you, I'll
find a wy."

"But you didna ken yoursel' that you should
have got the Hugh Blackadder?"

He would not let this depress him. "I ken
now," he said. Nevertheless, why he should have
got it was a mystery which he longed to fathom.
Mr. Ogilvy had returned to Glenquharity. so
that an explanation could not be drawn from him
even if he were willing to supply it, which was
improbable; but Tommy caught Grizel in the
Banker's close and compelled her to speak.

"I won't tell you a word of what Mr. Ogilvy
said," she insisted, in her obstinate way, and, oh,
how she despised Corp for breaking his promise.

"Corp didna ken he telled me," said Tommy,
less to clear Corp than to exalt himself. "I wrig-

499

gled it out o' him;" but even this did not bring Grizel to a proper frame of mind, so he said, to annoy her,

"At any rate you're fond o' me."

"I am not," she replied, stamping; "I think you are horrid."

"What else made you send Corp to me?"

"I did that because I heard you were calling yourself a blockhead."

"Oho," said he, "so you have been speiring about me though you winna speak to me!"

Grizel looked alarmed, and thinking to weaken his case, said, hastily, "I very nearly kept it from you, I said often to myself 'I won't tell him.'"

"So you have been thinking a lot about me!" was his prompt comment.

"If I have," she retorted, "I did not think nice things. And what is more, I was angry with myself for telling Corp to tell you."

Surely this was crushing, but apparently Tommy did not think so, for he said, "You did it against your will! That means I have a power over you that you canna resist. Oho, oho!"

Had she become more friendly so should he, had she shed one tear he would have melted immediately; but she only looked him up and down disdainfully, and it hardened him. He said with a leer, "I ken what makes you hold your hands so tight, it's to keep your arms frae wagging;" and

then her cry, "How do you know?" convicted
her. He had not succeeded in his mission, but
on his way home he muttered, triumphantly, "I
did her, I did her!" and once he stopped to ask
himself the question, "Was it because my heart
was in it?" It was their last meeting till they
were man and woman.

A blazing sun had come out on top of heavy
showers, and the land reeked and smelled as of the
wash-tub. The smaller girls of Monypenny were
sitting in passages playing at fivey, just as Sappho,
for instance, used to play it; but they heard the
Dubb of Prosen cart draw up at Aaron Latta's
door, and they followed it to see the last of Tommy
Sandys. Corp was already there, calling in at the
door every time he heard a sob; " Dinna, Elspeth,
dinna, he'll find a wy," but Grizel had refused to
come, though Tommy knew that she had been
asking when he started and which road the cart
would take. Well, he was not giving her a thought
at any rate; his box was in the cart now, and his
face was streaked with tears that were all for Elspeth. She should not have come to the door,
but she came, and — it was such a pitiable sight
that Aaron Latta could not look on. He went
hurriedly to his workshop, but not to warp, and
even the carter was touched and he said to Tommy,
" I tell you what, man, I have to go round by

Causeway End smiddy, and you and the crittur have time, if you like, to take the short cut and meet me at the far corner o' Caddam wood."

So Tommy and Elspeth, holding each other's hands, took the short cut and they came to the far end of Caddam, and Elspeth thought they had better say it here before the cart came; but Tommy said he should walk back with her through the wood as far as the Toom Well, and they could say it there. They tried to say it at the Well, but — Elspeth was still with him when he returned to the far corner of Caddam, where the cart was now awaiting him. The carter was sitting on the shaft, and he told them he was in no hurry, and what is more, he had the delicacy to turn his back on them and struck his horse with the reins for looking round at the sorrowful pair. They should have said it now, but first Tommy walked back a little bit of the way with Elspeth, and then she came back with him, and that was to be the last time, but he could not leave her, and so, there they were looking woefully at each other, and it was not said yet.

They had said it now, and all was over; they were several paces apart. Elspeth smiled, she had promised to smile because Tommy said it would kill him if she was greeting at the very end. But what a smile it was! Tommy whistled, he had promised to whistle to show that he was happy as long as Elspeth could smile. She stood still, but he went on, turning round every few yards to — to whistle. "Never forget, day nor night, what I said to you," he called to her. "You're the only one I love, and I care not a hair for Grizel."

But when he disappeared, shouting to her, " I'll find a wy, I'll find a wy," she screamed and ran after him. He was already in the cart, and it had started. He stood up in it and waved his hand to her, and she stood on the dyke and waved to him, and thus they stood waving till a hollow in the road swallowed cart and man and boy. Then Elspeth put her hands to her eyes and went sobbing homeward.

When she was gone, a girl who had heard all that had passed between them rose from among the broom of Caddam and took Elspeth's place on the dyke, where she stood motionless waiting for the cart to reappear as it climbed the other side of the hollow. She wore a black frock and a blue bonnet with white strings, but the cart was far away, and Tommy thought she was Elspeth, and springing to his feet again in the cart he waved and waved. At first she did not respond, for had she not heard him say "You're the only one I love, and I care not a hair for Grizel"? And she knew he was mistaking her for Elspeth. But by and by it struck her that he would be more unhappy if he thought Elspeth was too overcome by grief to wave to him. Her arms rocked passionately; no, no, she would not lift them to wave to him, he could be as unhappy as he chose. Then in a spirit of self-abnegation that surely raised her high among the daughters of men, though she was but a painted lady's child, she waved to him to save him pain, and he, still erect in the cart, waved back until nothing could be seen by either of them save wood and fields and a long, deserted road.

THE END